MW01131716

Watching Grace

A Grace Hanson Thriller

By L. G. Blankenship

This book is a work of fiction and any resemblance to any person, living or dead, places, events or localities are purely coincidental and are totally the author's imagination and used fictitiously.

Reviews! Reviews! Reviews!

Please take time to go back and leave a review. Indie authors live by the reviews they acquire, for marketing, publishing, sales and postings. The more favorable reviews an author has on their work the faster they climb the long ladder to being a bestselling author and have a place on the top 100.

Prologue

He stands in the dark shadows watching as she sits on her couch reading files, oblivious that there was someone just across the street with a perfect view of her whole apartment. He watches her as she cooks, as she undresses for bed, when she comes out of the shower. The perfect view and she didn't know it.

She tosses whatever she's reading down then leans back, rubbing her hands through her thick, long, wavy, dark brown hair. His hands twitch at the thought of touching that hair. Of touching the creamy, soft skin on her face, on her arms and legs, her body. He dreams of looking into her eyes, into her dark brown eyes.

She gets up, pacing the small room. She's agitated, has someone done something to her, is she mad at someone? She picks a piece of paper up from the floor reading it again before laying it back down on the coffee table. What is it? He had been holding back in following her, when they meet he wants it to be perfect. He wants her to see what he can do for her, he wants her to see her future. He wants her to know that she's special.

Adjusting the binoculars for a closer view he watches as she starts to unbutton her blouse, as she enters her bedroom. She goes into the bathroom cutting his view by closing the door. Does she sense someone watching her? Does she know he's there and being modest? Waiting patiently for her to come out he thinks of how happy she will be when they meet and he tells her that he can take care of her from now on.

The lights go out, he missed her coming from the bathroom, she's in bed now and he should be with her.

Frustrated he cries out in anger, now he must go and find a present, a present that will make him feel better, a present that will replenish him, a present that will show her how much he cares. He can feel the power of his knife as it slices through the skin and the muscle of someone's neck as he watches their life slowly drain from their bodies. He needs that power now.

Chapter 1

Sleeps eludes me. I get up with every intention of going into the office to study more files, instead I fix myself a pot of coffee pouring myself a gigantic cup before plopping down on the sofa to catch the early morning news.

I work as a profiler for the Boston Police Department, South Side. One of the busiest districts in Boston and it kept me hopping more than I like most of the time. Like right now the police have a serial killer and desperately trying to find the culprit before there are any more victims.

So far six bodies have been found in the last ten days, three women and three men. All thirty-two or close to it, all with well-paying high profile jobs, all athletic, all with dark brown hair and eyes. There are no other links between them, where they work or live, where they work out or friends in common. They even live in different parts of the

7

city. So what's the connection? With serial killers there is almost always a connection.

Keeping all this from the media has been a full time job within itself, but so far we've been successful. Flipping the TV to Channel 6, I take a sip of coffee waiting for the commercial to end to see what the top story is this morning. When the reporter comes on the sip of coffee I had just taken comes spewing out, turning the volume up, it can't be.

Standing in front of the Police Headquarters a reporter and one that is notorious for bending the truth and misleading with unverified facts. This is Anna Price with a story that has been kept from the citizens of Boston for several days now. It seems as if there may be a serial killer on the loose in town. So far there have been six victims that have had their throats cut and then their bodies dumped. At this time we don't know the location of where the brutal murders took place but we will update you with more on the Ghost Slasher as soon as we can. This is Anna Price reporting to you from downtown Boston.

Grabbing my phone, I call the captain to give him a heads up. As the phone rings I start flipping stations to see if any of the others were carrying the same story.

"Grace, do you have any idea what time it is?" Ah, the captain doesn't appear happy to be woken up at 4 am and will be less happy once I tell him.

"I know captain and I'm sorry. But I was just watching the news and Channel 6 was reporting on the murders, we now have a name, the Ghost Slasher."

Holding the phone away from my ear as he lets loose a volley of expletives that literally make me cringe. "Who leaked this? Who would do that? Get to the office as quick as you can!" I hear a loud bang and know that he's slammed his phone down.

Might as well go ahead and get to the office before it really hits the fan. After taking a quick shower and dressing in my boring outfit of cargo pants, a button down shirt and blazer, I pull my hair into a ponytail before stuffing my pockets with the necessities, grabbing my briefcase that had the files I was studying and leave my

apartment. Living only four blocks from the
station, I hardly ever drive to work and with the
nervous energy I was in possession of today I was
going to walk.

Before I even have a chance to get to my
office I'm called into the captain's office where I
find Detective Ron Webb and two other detectives
waiting. As the city's only profiler I was called
into most of the meetings that the captain had.

Captain George Pullen, 56 years old, thirty-
five years on the force. Tall, 6ft 3in, slim a good
guess is around 175 lbs with a full head of dark
grey hair, dark brown eyes that could scold with
just a look and he's still in tip top shape.
Clearing his throat. "Do we have any updates?
Please tell me you do because the governor wants
this closed, today."

I look over at Detective Ron Webb who is
suddenly interested in the floor, coward. 3rd Grade
Detective John Green clears his throat, he's
notorious for taking credit for any and everything
he can, and that's why he's 3rd grade and not 1st.

"Sir we have a few leads that we'll be following on today."

I snort which causes everyone turn to look at me. "No captain we don't have anything new, the same leads, the same lack of witnesses, the same lack of evidence. In other words not much of anything." Glaring at John when I finish speaking.

The captain sighs. "We have six that have died horrible deaths that we cannot find a reason for. Nor do we have a clue for a suspect. That about right?"

Being the brave one out of the group, I say. "Yes sir."

He stands glaring at everyone in turn before placing his hands on the desk and leans in. "Now I want to know who leaked the story to the press and I want to know now!"

This time it was John Green looking at the floor, even his partner was giving him the eye, but he doesn't fess up. I look over at Ron and see a look on his face that reminds me of a bull, it's clear he'd like to punch John in the face. Looking over at the captain, I can tell he believes its John too.

"Green I need you to wait outside my office for a minute. Everyone else is dismissed. Grace hold on."

Dang! Turning back around the captain motions for me to sit, once I was situated the captain starts talking. "Your intuition is usually right on with cases like this please tell me you have a feeling."

So Grace Hanson what are you going to tell the captain now? In the last ten days we've poured over the lives of the six people that have been killed. They all died horrific deaths, from strangulation, stabbed, burned and with their throats cut. Not one piece of evidence or DNA was found at any of the places where they were found. It's as if someone fell from the sky, killed then disappeared into nothingness.

There are no witnesses, no one heard or saw a thing, of course the neighborhoods that the crimes took place in are already high crime areas of the city so of course no one is going to volunteer information.

So what do I tell the captain? "Sir I'm sorry but right now, nothing."

His face clinches a little. The division was noted for closing major crimes fast, well it did before John Green and his partner joined them from Narcotics. Now they seem to be struggling to close even the minor cases. "Grace I'm asking you to be diligent, I'm giving Ron the lead on this, you two seem to work well together and right now I want Green as far away as possible. Please get out there and help solve this before the media starts making it worse than it already has." The captain stares at me for a second before smiling. "Trust me neither one will be anywhere close." Standing up he lays a hand on my shoulder. "Dig wherever you need to, if you and Ron need more hands just let me know and I'll get you the people."

I nod as I open the door to see John Green and his face was almost the same color as his last name. "Green inside!"

Oh to be a fly on the wall.

Finally making it into my office which was across the hall from the detectives, I toss my jacket on the small couch and lay my brief case on my desk before plopping down in my chair. Rubbing my face I turn toward the window gazing out at the overcast sky.

"So the pressures on."

I turn to find Detective Ron Webb standing in the doorway with two large cups of coffee. Holding my hand out I take one, inhaling the bitter aroma of the coffee before taking a sip. Most police stations were notorious for the bad coffee, but here, no it was almost perfect. "Yes it is. And right now I have no clue in which was to turn."

Ron sits down in one of the chairs that face my desk.

"Remind me again why I became a profiler, I keep forgetting." I meant that as a joke but Ron answers me.

"Well let's see, you wanted to be a psychologist, and then you wanted to be a police officer and a little criminal justice was thrown in there. So you got your degree, not once but twice then got your badge before you decided you wanted to be a profiler where you went to Quantico for a year. I call that not being able to make your mind up." Propping his feet on the corner if my desk.

Twisting the cup of coffee in my hands thinking he's right, I couldn't make my mind up on what I really wanted to do. All I was sure of was that I like talking to people, I like solving problems and I like to figure a puzzle out. What I didn't like was talking to one person for an hour that wouldn't respond to you and I was never comfortable chasing criminals or consoling victims. So I compromised, I have my degree in psychology so I could open a private practice if I wanted I also have a degree in criminal justice. I still carry my badge; officially I was employed by the Boston Police Department and I still carry a weapon. But I didn't want to be on the streets, so I guess I could have a desk job. The profiling was suggested to me by my trainer at the Police Academy and it fits. It has everything I like to do and if I must say so myself, I'm good at it.

"I hate it when you're right." Turning to face Ron. "Seriously nothing came in last night?"

Shaking his head in answer, he was a man of few words.

I pull the six files from my briefcase stacking them in the order of their deaths. "I reread everything last night hoping that we missed something the first time but still nothing jumped out."

Ron sits quietly sipping his coffee while studying my face. He was a good looking man of medium height, with dark blonde hair that always needed a trim, eyes that were the color of light mocha and built like the linebacker he was in college. I don't think I've ever seen him in a suit, he's partial to jeans or cargos and tee shirts with an over shirt to hide his weapon. A totally relaxed human being.

"If you don't mind I'd like to put everything up and walk through a timeline." He suggests and I knew he meant to get a whiteboard out and start placing everything in order. Which usually brought out another avenue to try.

I nod at him that I agreed, grabbing the files so we could use the white board in the abandoned conference room at the end of the hall. Before we began we had to clean the files from the last case. Reading the first captioned picture it was dated 1994, so this hasn't been used in thirteen years. "Do we need to box all this up or shred it?" I ask not sure of past procedure.

He looks at the date stamps before tossing it in a large box on the floor. "Box it then records can deal with it."

Sounded like a plan to me so we toss everything in the box then began with victim number one.

Chapter 2

To me it was a little easier to call them victims at first until I got to know them and before we would be done I would know them intimately.

Victim one was a male, age 32, lived alone on High Street in the second floor apartment of a townhouse. He was an IT tech for the NE Medical Center. He had dark brown hair, brown eyes, by appearances worked out regularly and was 6'3". By his bulk and height he should have been able to at least subdue his attacker enough to get away. His financials show him to be very conservative in his spending and the search of his apartment showed the most expensive thing he owned was the entertainment set-up which included three hi-def flat screens, an X-box, an extremely high tech sound system and a computer.

He had no girlfriend, his friends said he was interested in the Game of Conquest and could play tirelessly for hours. He was a member of Crown Gym on Congress Street and appeared to work out three random nights a week. Other than that the man had never even had a speeding ticket.

Victim two a female, age 33, lived alone on Pearl Street worked at the post office three blocks from her home, she was a postal inspector, very lucrative job for one so young. She was 5'9", very slim but well toned, another one that worked out regularly. Dark brown hair and eyes with a light sprinkling of freckles across her nose. She was another that was careful with their money and her home was sparsely furnished and again several hi-def flat screens and a high tech sound system, but no X-box but there were quite a few games on her laptop including Game of Conquest.

Victim three a male, age 32, lived with two other males on Beach Street near Chinatown in a large townhouse. Worked at Raicon as a programmer, another lucrative job. He was 6'1" and again worked out regularly at a gym in Chinatown. Dark brown hair and eyes, very careful with his money but had some credit card debt. His home was sparsely furnished but there was an entire room with five hi-def flat screens there was an X-box and a Wii along with several laptops connected, also the Game of Conquest. This one didn't work out but was still well toned and trim.

Victim four a female, age 32, lived with her sister on West Street and worked at the courthouse as a court clerk, very well paid position here. Dark brown hair and eyes she was 5'8" and a runner. She had been in the Boston Marathon several times and came in third at the last race. Her finances were somewhat normal for someone her age, a couple of credit cards with minimal balances, she drove a used Toyota that was paid for. The home had been their parents until they passed away leaving the sisters with a paid place of residence. Again the flat screen TV's but no Game of Conquest this time, but we haven't found her computer yet.

Victim five a male, age 33, lived alone on Water Street and worked at home as a website designer, making a very good living from it. Dark brown hair and eyes he was 6', a little heavy around the middle but otherwise in good shape. Minor credit card debt and again the TV set up, but no game consoles. But he liked old movies and frequented the cinema in South Market regularly.

Victim six a female, age 32, lived alone in a duplex on Hawley Street and was part owner of a dress boutique near the Old South. Didn't own a vehicle and appeared to walk everywhere. Very athletic, had a membership at a gym at the Old South Meeting house. Dark hair and eyes, she was 5'9" a little on the thin side. Minimal debt and only one flat screen in the home but two laptops and no gaming equipment.

Getting their information on the white board, I stand back. The first thing I had noticed they all live on the south side, all fairly close to work. Three were involved in gaming, three weren't. All were in good shape, four lived alone, and two didn't. They all had different career fields none were in serious debt. So what was the connection?

Chapter 3

Sitting on the edge of the table, reading each again and again, Ron puts the picture of each one at the head of the columns I had made. None of their faces had any damage so the pictures made them appear to be sleeping.

The only thing that kept nagging me was the fact that they all lived on the south side, so did I. I lived in a converted factory building that had been made into twenty apartments. I had a one bedroom on the top floor that was tiny by most standards but was perfect for me. My neighbors were a few other abandoned buildings that were being renovated for other apartments, several small factories and a few stores peppered the area.

Each victim had been found in a different place again on the south side, two had been at the docks, one at the underground parking lot, one close to the Boston Tea party site one at the park behind the post office, one at an abandoned baseball field. None had been killed where they were found. No DNA, no evidence, nothing, nada, zilch had been found at any of the sites. No tire tracks, no drag marks, no blood spatter, it was as if each victim had literally been dropped where they were found.

"Ron do we have a large map of the city?"

"We should. Let me ask Sheila, she'll know." Sheila was the receptionist slash secretary slash ruler of the office, she knew where everything was, where everyone was and everything that was going on.

Ten minutes later Ron was back waving a large tube of paper in his hand. "Told you she would know."

Spreading the map out on the table, I could see that it wasn't going to work lying flat so I tape it to the opposite wall. Taking a different colored marker for each victim placing a mark at their address and then where their bodies were found. Standing back, no pattern was there, yet.

Pulling the interviews with the friends and families from the files I lay them in order on the table. There was only one page for two of the victims, there was no family and apparently few friends for them. As Ron starts reading the interviews out loud I stand in front of the picture of victim as he reads. This is where I start to get to know them and start calling them by name.

"Evan Littell was pretty much a loner as his friends say, he preferred to stay home when he wasn't at work or the gym. As far as they know he's never had a steady girlfriend but has dated in the past. Recently they say he's been holed up with the new version of Game of Conquest determined to get to level one hundred, whatever that means. He's considered a genius at work, but no one knew him very well. Was always on time didn't complain about working overtime and went out of his way to help with anything and the man has not had a vacation since he started working for the medical center six years ago. Wow talk about no life."

"Ron! The man was killed." Really could psychoanalyze him, but I'd be afraid of my diagnosis.

"Sorry." He lays Evan's file aside. "Andrea Spencer, considered lofty by her friends, said she wasn't into partying or going out but liked to go to comic con's and never missed a Star Trek or Star Wars movie. One friend stated that she was into the Game of Conquest but wasn't obsessed with winning levels. They did say she was determined to lift 250lbs. Wow. I don't think I could do that." He clears his throat. "No one that was canvassed in the neighborhood knew anything about her except that she was quiet and kept to herself."

As Ron talked about each victim, I study their picture imagining their lives. By Evan's curly, unruly hair he gave the appearance of being a little bit of a loner. Andrea on the other hand looked like a model and by looks I would place her at the center of attention with the professional haircut, sculpted brows with a perfectly shaped nose and chin. She didn't give the look of being a geek that loved games and comics.

"Terrance Chow, of Asian descendants but both sides of his family have been born in America for several decades. Friends say he was always talking whether anyone was within earshot or not. Would do sit-ups and crunches while he watched TV and wasn't interested in winning when he played games. One friend said he liked to watch several ball games at the same time that's why all the TV's were set up together. His work colleagues said he was always courteous, always pleasant and brilliant when it came to programming and working out bugs in software. Wasn't interested in going out unless it was to a game and loved the Red Sox. No steady girlfriend. Neighbors said he was always friendly and the only noise they ever heard was cheering." Ron looks at me. "I know they're all victims, but I'm starting to feel a little sorry for them just because of their lifestyles."

Turning to face him, I ask. "Ron describe a normal day for you."

He rubs his chin before answering. "Okay. I get up fix coffee, check the news and come into work. If nothing major has happened we work on cold cases or do interviews. After work I either stop and pick up take out or eat out then go home and watch a movie or a game…." A blush fills his cheeks. "Shut up Ron and get back to work."

Turning back around so he doesn't see my smile. People tend to think if you're a certain age you should be bar hopping, hanging with friends every night, going out to concerts, to the movies, whatever. Truth is no matter what age you are more nights are spent home alone or with your significant other watching TV or reading than going out. Boring? No, comfortable, secure, safe, normal.

"Hope Shelby another one that worked out only she liked to run. Canvasses state that she ran everywhere, several neighbors have gone to the marathon in the past to root her on. Walked to work even though she had a car, her co-workers state she was always on time, never complained but kept to herself. Her sister said she had few friends and they liked to get together sometimes to watch horror movies but that she seldom if ever went out. She also stated that Hope was a daddy's girl and when he passed away from cancer she was devastated. Has never had a steady boyfriend and rarely if ever dates.

Hope was an attractive woman, her face was a little chubby for a runner though so I would think

27

her running was more for weight control. Her dark hair appears to be a little curly and there was a long scar that ran from her ear to her chin. "Ron make a note to ask her sister how Hope got the scar."

"Roger that." I watch as he scribbles in his notebook. "Ready" I nod.

"Robert Glesson, called Rob by friends, lived in one of those converted brownstones in the bottom apartment. Worked from home, the living room had six computers set up along with four laptops on the opposite wall were three flat screens and an extensive library of movies the latest being made in 1960. No close friends, no girlfriend and the neighbors describe him as friendly and extremely quiet.

As Ron read I jotted more notes to the victim's profile, waiting for something to pop out, not necessarily a clue but something that could tie all six victims together.

Sandra Phillips, lived near the Old South, her business was just starting to take off. Her partner says that she was outgoing, never sat still and could work twenty four hours straight without blinking an eye. No vehicle and her duplex is eight blocks from work. She had a membership at the Old South gym. You know that one concentrates more on boxing and fighting. Neighbors only knew that she was always on the go but always polite, one stated that she helped her retrieve her cat that had gotten out. No boyfriend but had recently had several dates with a man, but her business partner said that Sandra wasn't very impressed and had broken their last two dates.

Ron stretches, lacing his fingers behind his head. "Anything popping out yet?"

"No." Each one of the victims were attractive, each one had taken care of themselves. Each one except for Terrance and Hope all lived alone, close to work and most walked to work. "Okay keep going." Picking the marker back up I stand in front of Evan gazing at his face as Ron starts.

"Evan graduated with top honors from Harvard. Born and raised in Boston proper, both parents were killed by a drunk driver four years ago. No siblings and no close relatives. He's considered a genius with an IQ of 170."

I nod. "He was a genius."

Moving to Andrea. "She graduated from Harvard again considered a genius, her IQ is 169, her father died when she was a teenager from a heart attack her mother passed away last year from cancer. Born and raised in Boston proper." I hear papers shuffling before Ron clears his throat. "Terrance graduated from MIT at the age of 20, IQ was 173 born and raised in Chinatown, his father was killed in a gang altercation three years ago, his mother is in a home in Prospect with severe dementia."

Leaning back against the table, on the surface each one had the picture perfect lives but underneath it seems like tragedy had touched all their lives. I move to the fourth victim as Ron starts talking.

"Hope and her sister were born and raised in the Clements area, both went to Yale. Her mother had MS most of her life passing away five years ago, her father died from a heart attack a year later." Ron takes a drink of water before picking up the next file. "Robert went to Harvard but seems to have been an average student. Born and raised in Boston proper, no siblings, mother left when he was a child his father raised him alone but passed away last year from complications from an arterial graft."

I move to the last victim. "Last one. Sandra was born and raised in Boston proper, went to Boston City College. Her mother died while on a missionary trip to Uganda, her father moved to Utah afterwards but her partner said she hasn't had any contact with him."

I sit down looking at what we had so far.

Chapter 4

Getting up from the chair he had been glued to, Ron moves to the board. "There's no connection between any of them. Nothing in common but their ages and coloring."

"I know. This one is going to be hard." Looking at my watch, wow it was past 2pm no wonder my stomach was complaining. "Let's go get some lunch I'm starving."

"Good idea. Do we lock the room?"

"Yes I don't want John Green even thinking about coming in here." As Ron goes to get the key to the room from Shelia, I gather the files and just to be safe pull the projection screen down to cover the white board.

Ron comes back dangling the key as I walk from the room. After locking and pocketing the key we return to my office where I dump the files. Locking my door behind me we leave the office by the side door which opens into the lobby of the courthouse. Crossing the lobby to the other side door that opens into an alley, we walk in silence until we reach the street. Standing on the corner waiting on traffic I get a creepy feeling. Was someone watching us? Feeling the hair on my neck tingling, I reach up to rub my neck as I look around.

Nothing unusual. People walking down the sidewalk, most with their eyes glued to their cell phones. People waiting to cross the street, going into businesses and stores. I didn't see anything out of the ordinary but I still felt as if we were being watched.

We cross the street, entering the diner that most of the occupants in the courthouse frequent. The place was packed as usual but we manage to find a table in the back close to the kitchen. Perfect for conversation because no one could hear us over the kitchen noise.

After ordering we wait for the waitress to bring our drinks before talking. I watch Ron as we wait, he of course took the chair with his back to the wall. His light brown eyes were taking in the other customers with just a hint of a frown on his broad forehead. His hair was a little longer than most detectives in the office but he kept it well trimmed. With a face that was a little chubby it gave him that perpetual little boy look, but his chin was well defined as was his nose.

The linebacker body was thick and muscular leaving him with just a hint of having a neck but I knew the man could outrun most everyone on the force. He was a good friend and colleague, I'd never had any other feelings for him and probably never would, there just wasn't anything there.

Feeling his eyes on me I turn my attention away, taking a sip of my drink I lean forward a little. "I'd like to go to their homes and then where each one was found."

Ron nods at me. "Good idea. Want to start first thing in the morning? I'd like to read the medical examiner's report when we get back."

"You do that, giving me the basic of details please." I wasn't really squeamish I just don't want to hear the gory details unless it was absolutely necessary.

With a smile he says. "Sure about that? Could be very interesting."

"I'm sure. We need to get the time of death on each one and try to figure what they could have been doing and where. We know they were all moved after death so somewhere close is a possibility. There are so many abandoned factories and buildings on the south side it would be almost impossible to search each one."

The waitress slides our plates in front of us, mine was a BLT with chips and extra pickles. Ron's was a turkey pastrami club with fries. We're quiet as we eat not because we were starving and didn't want to talk but because a woman and her young son has sat at the table right across from us. No more shop talk.

><

Waiting at the entrance to the bank for the next present, they were later than normal leaving for lunch. He had been watching the present for a few days now and they were everything he needed. They weren't as tall as the others but their dark hair was so nice. They always went to the gym right after work and stayed for two hours coming out sweaty and tired. Where were they? He'd need to move the car before long or it'll attract attention. The door to the bank opens, he stiffens ready to pull him close with the syringe in his hand, once they're clear of the door he clamps his hand on the gift's shoulder. "Derrick how are you man?" When the gift turns he plunges the syringe into their side, guiding them to his car as the gift starts to stumble. Slamming the car door, he looks around making sure no one was paying attention to what he was doing. Smiling at his ingenuity and the present, she was going to be so pleased.

><

We finish our meals chatting about nothing but saying everything. Ron told me about the break up with his latest girlfriend. He went through women faster than most men change their underwear. I knew it was because he was focusing on being the center of a woman's life, I had tried to talk to him several times but his response was 'I know what I want doc' so I let it go until he was ready to listen.

Flipping a coin to see who got to pick the check up, which this time was me, Ron leaves a generous tip, smiles at the little boy across from us, hand slaps a couple of men as he passes then opens the door for me. Never said he wasn't a gentleman.

Walking the long way back to the station I pay attention to everything going on around me, it was a habit that I couldn't let go of.

I was born in Boston, lived in Boston my whole life. When I was a child we lived on the North Side, we had a tiny brownstone and I mean tiny it was sixteen feet wide, four stories high, each floor had two rooms, a narrow hallway and a stairwell. There was a postage stamp sized front yard that I stayed in as much as possible.

Across the street lived my best friend, her name was Stella, her family had moved to Boston from New York but they were originally from Serbia and there were always strange men coming and going from their house. One day Stella and I were in my front yard playing with dolls when I noticed a large black car turn the corner and park. No one got out which I thought was strange so I said something to Stella about it. She shrugged saying there were always strange cars parking there, I had never noticed. She said she had to go now so she walked across the street glancing at the car as she went inside and shut the door. I never saw Stella or her family again. I later found out that her parents had been killed execution style at the piers, Stella was never spoken of or seen again. So now I pay attention to everything going on around me.

Ron was quiet as we walked back while I was more or less concentrating on my surroundings. Watching as people came out of stores, people passing each other on the street. I stop and back up against a building, Ron looks at me with a frown but joins me.

There was a coffee shop across the street, a busy coffee shop. People were going in and out at a fast clip, my eyes latch onto a young dark haired female juggling her cell, a briefcase and her purse as she opens the door. Counting silently to myself to time her, a minute and forty six seconds later she comes out now juggling her cell, her briefcase, her purse and a cup of coffee. Anyone could have easily bumped into her, they could have ripped her purse from her, they could even grab her by the arm and pull her into the closest alley. Could that have been the way our perp caught his prey?

Pushing away from the building I continue walking down the street, Ron in step beside me. "Are you thinking that this is totally random and the victims were picked up off the street?"

"Possibility. Only if they were on the street, but the victim could have screamed to draw attention to them."

"Unless it was late at night. We have victims that were athletes, they went to the gym, most likely at night or they ran, again most likely at night. Also they all lived within walking distance or next door to stores and markets, what's to say after they got home and changed or checked their mail they went back out to the store."

I nod. "All good possibilities. Let's get the time of death that will give us an idea. I'd like to talk to their friends again too."

Holding the door to the courthouse for me, we enter to hear a loud commotion coming from the police entrance. Ron hustles to see what was going while I take the side entrance into the station.

Once in my office I line the six files on my desk, opening the first one, flipping through the pages for the ME's report but it wasn't there, the other five files didn't have one either. What the?

Calling the ME's office I tell the secretary what I was looking for, putting me on hold, I tap my fingers waiting, listening to the canned music. The music stops and a rough male voice comes on the line. "Grace?"

"Hello Dr. Mellon. I was wondering if I could have a copy of each of the six victims. The files I have the ME report doesn't appear to be included."

"There's a reason for that. Come down here and I'll explain."

Chapter 5

Hanging the phone up I gather the files heading for the stairwell to take me to the basement. Once I was in the basement I take the corridor that leads under the courthouse building, someone once measured the distance of all the hallways down here, there's eight miles of concrete incased hallways with everything from storage rooms, offices, a few extra holding cells and the morgue.

Pushing open the double glass doors to the morgue I smile thinking of everyone's reaction when they come in, wrinkling their noses, pinching them shut, holding a tissue under their nose, but the odor had never bothered me, it was what was under the white sheets.

Seeing Dr. Mellon through the glass windows of his office, I knock before pushing the door open. "Dr. Mellon. You had some information for me?"

"Grace. Good to see you. Please have a seat."

Taking one of the padded chairs in front of his desk, I cross my arms over the files I was holding and wait for the doctor.

"The reports on the six victims have been held back." Holding his hands up. "Now I can't tell you why but I can give you a copy of the pertinent information, that is." He wags his finger a little. "You don't share the information or let anyone know that you have it." He starts to hand me a folder but holds it back a little. "And no putting anything on that white board you use either."

With a smile. "Of course not, I will do as you wish. Thank you so much." I start flipping through the papers. "But why hold the information back… ah, I bet I know, the leak in the office."

Dr. Mellon smiles at me as he laces his fingers across his round belly. "Always said you were too smart to for your own good, but yes that's pretty much it. So you see why I don't want you scribbling your thoughts on that board you like to use."

Nodding my understanding. "Of course, you have way too much valuable information for me to get on your bad side." Scanning down Evan's report. "Can you tell me if you found any needle marks on any of the victims?"

Furrowing his forehead. "No. I wondered the same thing a couple of the victims were very well muscled and should have been able to defend themselves. But I didn't find a thing of course some of the stab wounds could have been over a puncture mark. Sadly there's no way to tell for sure. But I can tell you that there were no drugs or toxins."

Okay so there went that theory. "I'm sure I'll have a few questions after I read the reports."

"You come on back and we'll knock our heads together."

"Thanks doctor."

Giving his secretary a nod goodbye as I leave clutching the reports to my chest as I make my way back to my office, except when I open the door to the police station a commotion is still going on. Stopping at my office first, I tuck the reports the doctor had given me into my desk, locking the door behind me before heading to the center of the room to find out what was going on.

Seeing the captain across the room I make my way to stand behind him. "What's going on?"

"John Green. He and the reporter that gave that report last night are having words. Yes I'm letting them because John's already said a couple of things that implicate him as being the leak."

Just then John steps to the reporter's face and screams at her. "You're under arrest for harassment." Luckily before John could grab her arm a couple of officers step in and pull him away.

The captain makes his way over to the reporter leaning close to her ear before leading her to his office and shutting the door. Oh to be that fly on the wall.

Feeling a little sorry for John that he made such a spectacle of himself but he always puts himself in these positons.

Since the action was over I return to my office to find Ron leaning against the door. "Wasn't that interesting? Did you hear him tell her she jumped the gun?"

"I did." I unlock my door going straight for my desk to get the files. "He just pretty much cooked himself out there."

Ron gets comfortable in the chair in front of my desk. "Yep."

Laying the files out in order and then pulling out what Dr. Mellon had given me. "Okay I have the ME's reports and this has to be between us." I raise my eyebrows to get the point across.

Ron nods his understanding as he pulls his little notebook and pen from his pocket.

Pulling each report and laying them on top of the corresponding file, I start with the first one. "COD was multiple stab wounds to the abdomen perforating the stomach wall and two arteries. Other wounds consisted of burns to the chest, attempted strangulation, knife slashes on the throat, broken bones in the right hand, bruises on the torso, upper thighs, back and face." Reading further. "Time of death is estimated between 2 and 4 am."

The only thing Ron says is, "Um."

"Number two, COD multiple stab wounds to the abdomen, arteries severed, burns, strangulation, knife slashes on the throat, broken bones in both feet, bruises over entire torso and face. Time of death between 11 pm and 2 am. Number three, COD same, burns, knife slashes, broken bones in both hands, bruises on torso and face. Time of death between 1 and 3 am." Taking a breath. "Number four, COD same, all the same except for broken bones in both feet and hands and a broken jaw. Time of death between 12 am and 5 am." I look up to see Ron's face set in stone. "Number five, COD same, all the rest the same, both legs broken, time of death between 2 and 5 am." Picking up the last report. "Number six. COD one stab wound to the abdomen, no burns, no strangulation, but this one has a broken back, time of death between 11 pm and 3 am." Tossing the last report in the desk, I rub my eyes trying to get the visions of the horrific deaths out of my head.

"I see a couple of things here, the men were killed later or earlier in the morning, they all seemed to have fought back with broken bones in their hands and feet."

Nodding at his statement. "I asked Dr. Mellon if they could have been drugged, I mean a couple of these guys were really well toned, anyway he said he didn't find any puncture marks and nothing in their blood work."

Without raising his head from his notes Ron says. "Puncture marks could have been under the stab wounds or under a bruise. If they were given something just mild enough to knock them out to get them to where they were tortured it could have worn off by the time the doc took samples."

My eyes snap to Ron's face. "And how could we find that out?"

Shrugging his shoulders. "No way now, too late. I hope this doesn't jinx things but if there's another victim, we need to test them as soon as we find them."

I nod at what he said, but I was so hoping there weren't anymore victims. But if this was a serial killer, there would be more, maybe many more.

Rubbing my face. "Okay let's call it a day. Tomorrow we'll go walking." I try to smile but it wasn't in me.

Ron gives me a nod before pushing out of the chair, tucking his little notebook away and leaving.

Now this is where I start getting a little deranged, a little movie will start playing in my head of each victim and the way they died, sleep will be almost impossible.

Chapter 6

Leaving the building by the side alley door making sure it shuts behind me, I walk to the back of the building with every intention of stopping at the store for at least ten pounds of coffee.

Reaching my building I look around, the feeling of being watched was there. The little hairs on the back of my neck were twitching. Acting as normal as possible I shift my shopping bag to unlock the main door to my building making sure it locks behind me. Taking a glance around I don't see anyone watching or paying attention to me. Deciding I didn't want to trust the elevator tonight I take the stairs to the top floor.

There are only three apartments on my floor, one was empty and the other was occupied by John Benjamin, a retired accountant who pretty much kept to himself but knew if I banged on the wall or screamed he'd be there in a heartbeat.

Unlocking my door I get the creepy feeling of being watched again. Setting my bags down, letting the strap to my briefcase slide down my arm, I reach behind me for my weapon. Taking slow quiet steps I peep around the corner to the kitchen, clear. Looking toward my bedroom door which was partially closed, slowly I push the door all the way open. Nothing, I check the bathroom before looking into the double closet and for good measure look under the bed too.

Letting out the breath I didn't realize I was holding, I tuck my weapon in the nightstand drawer before pulling my jacket off. Going into the closet I change clothes, emptying my pockets in the little tray I kept by the closet door.

In the bathroom I wash my face before pulling my hair back into a ponytail. Feeling a little more refreshed I unpack the few groceries I had purchased then make a huge pot of coffee. In my mind I knew it was going to be a long night.

Since my apartment was so small I use my coffee table as my desk. Pulling the files out I lay them on the corner of the table before grabbing the remote, turning the TV on more for company than to watch.

Pouring myself a large mug of coffee, I take a sip as I make myself comfortable on the couch. Picking the first file up, I lean back propping my feet on the table. Now to get really acquainted with the victims.

After reading three files, I toss the one I was holding down needing a break. Getting up I stretch the kinks out as I head to the kitchen for another mug of coffee. Rubbing my neck, those tiny little hairs were giving me the creepy feeling of being watched again.

><

Ah my pretty, you are home early tonight, such a pleasure that is! But see a little sadness on your face. Don't worry though there is another present for you. Hoping you like what I've done this time. One day you will be the only dark haired beauty, you will be the princess, you will be revered and you will be all mine. All mine. He has to get closer to her!

He yells in happiness accidentally dropping his binoculars to the street below. Oh no! How will he watch her now? He must fix this, quickly, he has to keep an eye on his precious.

><

Carrying my mug to the coffee table, I set it down before walking to the window. Looking out all I see is the roof of the building next door and beyond that other buildings. That was one of the drawbacks of living in the old manufacturing district there wasn't much of a view unless you like looking at brick.

Still with the creepy feeling, I pull the drapes shut and take a deep breath. This had to be the case that was starting to freak me out.

Sitting back down I start on victim four turning the TV to a comedy, the sound of canned laughter helped, some.

Three hours and two mugs of coffee later I rub my eyes pulling my hair loose then running my hands through it. There was absolutely no point in even trying to lie down. Sleep would evade me for several nights. So a nice hot shower and then start with my evaluation of each victim. I won't start calling them by name until they catch the murderer and that's all you can call him, a murderer. I have come to the conclusion that it is a man though, it would take a man to subdue some of the victims. A very muscular, very powerful man. Probably 6'2" or better with most of his power in his arms and chest.

In the shower I run the areas of town the victims came from on a mental map. Slamming the water off, I stand there dripping water for a minute before grabbing a towel and drying myself off. Tossing on cargos and a tee shirt slipping my feet into runners then filling my pockets and tucking my weapon in the holster at the small of my back, I grab my keys, making sure the door was locked behind me.

Running down the stairs and out the front door, I call Ron as I jog back to the courthouse. No answer. Leaving him a message just as I unlock the side door to the building.

Taking the stairs two at a time I bypass my office and go to the old conference room. Drat! The door was locked and Ron has the key. Turning in a circle, what to do, what to do? Looking at the lock again, I go to my office unlock the door then rummage in my desk for a couple of giant paper clip. Ah ha! Finding two, I straighten the ends out as I go back down the hall. Slipping one end in the lock, I twist with the other until I hear it click. Thank you YouTube.

Turning on the light I walk to the map focusing on the marks I had put there earlier. Taking a pencil I join all the dots then draw a circle around the whole thing. There were going to be three more murders.

Chapter 7

Ron finds me sitting in front of the map the next morning. "What are you doing?"

Swinging the chair around to face him. "There's going to be three more and I have a pretty good idea where he's going to be searching for the victims."

Ron plops down in a chair, leaning back with a look of disbelief on his face. "And how may I ask do you know that?"

"This man, and yes I have come to the conclusion it is a man, likes the less populated areas of the city that's why it's been focused on the south side. Besides the tourist attractions the population is mostly millennials living in reconverted factories, buildings and brownstones. All the victims were either found in abandoned one story buildings or on streets that are pretty much quiet all day and night." I get up and run my finger around the marks I had made. "This is where all the victims lived." Running my finger around the area the victims were found. "This is where they were found. See anything?"

I sit back down as Ron studies the map before shaking his head. "No not really."

Putting my finger on each mark, I slowly move my finger. "If he gets three more victims, that will be six more marks on the map. If you connect them all, it's a pentagram, or a five sided star." Turning my focus back to Ron. "I'm not saying that he's involved in wiccan or any kind of cult, it just seems that it's following a pattern."

"It could be a badge." Ron says.

Studying the map again. Yipes it could be a badge, our badges were five sided stars in a circle at least mine was since I'm considered an administrative officer. "Jeez, that changes my outlook a little." But the patrol officers and detectives badges were oblong shields. So maybe not a badge. I rub my head. "Ready to go walking?"

"Sure you're up to it? Looks like you've been up all night."

"Yeah I have but I never can sleep when I'm on a case. Trust me once I have two or three hundreds ounces of coffee I'll be fine." I head for my office to get my tape recorder and camera before we head out.

Taking the elevator to the first floor, I make a pit stop at the tiny coffee kiosk that was in the lobby. Looking at Ron. "Coffee?"

"Not right now, thanks."

Paying for my extra-large black coffee, I take a sip and instantly feel better. Nothing like a jolt of caffeine to chase away any brain cobwebs. Pushing through the glass double doors of the courthouse I groan. "Wow sunshine." Putting my sunglasses on as we start our trek.

"Okay explain to me why you think it's a pattern."

Swallowing the sip of coffee I had taken. "Most serial killers are concise. They have their plan mapped out in their mind, they are precise, they study their victims, they stalk them, they imagine what will happen once they have them. They very seldom leave evidence which makes it so hard to apprehend them but they stick with a plan. A plan that usually is in their comfort zone, whether

57

it's where they work, they live, grew up, a place that has meaning to them. So we're going to walk around where the victims lived and worked then where they were found. There's a link there and we need to find it hopefully before the next victim."

Ron's quiet as we walk, hopefully digesting what I had explained. I stay focused on my surroundings as we enter the street where the first victim lived.

It was close to the harbor so the scent of warm water, fish and maybe a little whiff of garbage since the trash barges make daily treks up and down the harbor. Standing across the street I watch the pattern of the people, there weren't many out since this was a residential street, but the few that were are young professionals. The closest alley was a block away, there were no abandoned buildings close, the businesses were small groceries, clothing shops, a shoe store, a couple of restaurants and coffee shops, a very nice place to live.

I try to put myself in the killer's shoes, where would be the best place to abduct someone?

Leaning back against the wall of a clothing shop, I watch and study. But I was thinking that the first victim wasn't taken here, so it must have been at his job.

We continue on to two more of the victims homes, but I was coming to the same conclusion, they weren't taken from their homes.

Ron had been really quiet during our whole walk. "What's wrong?"

Creasing his forehead. "Nothing just watching you, trying to see what you were seeing."

"And?"

"I don't think they were taken from their homes or close. Their jobs would be too busy, too many people, too congested, but if they were followed maybe they had a pattern of going somewhere often, maybe a bar or nightclub?"

Nodding at his statement. "You're right, that's exactly what I was thinking. But our victims weren't known for going out much, they were pretty reclusive. But most of them had something in common, video games and electronic equipment."

Stopping in his tracks. "You think an electronics store?"

"No, so far I've only seen three on our walk and none were close to any of the residences. We need to find out where they purchased their equipment."

Just as Ron opens his mouth his phone rings, pulling it from his pocket. "It's the captain." Answering the phone. "Yes sir." Rubbing his hands over his face. "We'll be right there." Sliding his phone back in his pocket he raises a hand for a cab that stops in front of us. "We need to get to the hospital. A man just walked in saying he'd been kidnapped."

We keep quiet in the cab, but my mind was racing, if this man had been a victim and got away, we may have just gotten lucky enough to find out who the murderer is.

Chapter 8

The cab lets us out at the emergency door, there were patrol cars filling the parking lot along with a few black SUV's. The double glass doors slide open as we approach, walking into a chaos of police officers and hospital workers.

The captain breaks away from the doctor he was talking to. "Detective, Grace."

"Captain. Can we talk to this man?" I was hoping that he was able to give us some information, quickly.

The captain nods. "Oh you can talk to him, matter of fact it's getting him to slow down that's been the problem. Follow me." He leads us down a hall passing all the small cubicles you find in any emergency room to a door guarded by a patrol officer. Nodding to the captain the officer opens the door, letting all three of us in.

Once inside we see Detective Johannson leaning against the wall, his arm resting on a shelf attached to the wall. When he sees the captain enter, relief washes over his face as he straightens up. "Captain."

"You can go Johannson." The captain nods as the detective slides past us, quickly.

The captain stands in front of the man that was sitting on the side of a gurney. He had a small bandage over his right eye, several large bruises were covering the rest of his face. His hand was clasped over his stomach as if in pain, but it was the fury in his eyes that made my blood start pumping faster. He knew.

"Sir this is Detective Ron Webb and Grace Hanson, they would like to talk to you if you don't mind."

"Be glad to if it helps catch that crazy lunatic."

The captain nods at us before leaving the room. I turn back to the man, holding my hand out. "I'm Grace Hanson." Nodding at his stomach. "What other injuries did you sustain?"

The man snorts. "Well let's see. I have several broken ribs, my face was used as a punching bag, I was hit in the head and I think they said I had a slight concussion. Oh let's not forget whatever the hell the drug was he gave me."

Ron nods before speaking. "I'm Detective Webb but please call me Ron and your name sir?" He has his trusty little notebook out ready to write.

"Jeffrey Owens. I'm the loan officer at City Bank on Colony."

Colony Street was considered South Side by a stretch of the imagination and much busier. "Would you mind going over what happened again for us?" I sit down in the one chair that was in the room, hoping that Ron wouldn't mind, but I see him taking the position the last detective chose, leaning against the wall.

"Sure. I was going to lunch it was 12:50 when I looked at the clock. When I opened the doors a man clapped his hand on my shoulder and said something like 'Hey man how are you' then I felt a sting in my side. The man pulled me toward his car that was parked at the curb pushing me in the back seat."

I hold my finger up. "Can you describe him and the car please."

"Well it was quick but I guess he was average height, he was shorter than me and I'm 6ft. Maybe about your height." He looks at me.

"I'm 5'10' so he was shorter than you?"

"Yes and slim. Not skinny but slim. But I did notice that he had a lot of hand strength to pull me toward the car." Jeffrey looks at me and I nod for him to continue. "He had one of those hoodies on that all the kids like now, dark grey. I didn't notice any emblems or mottos on it. It covered his whole face, I could only make out a shadow." This is what I wanted, for him to go back to that time, his voice was taking on a soft tone as he remembers. "The car, I remember it stunk like stale food and the car was old. Maybe ten years or better, a Chevrolet, one of those small ones, oh I can't remember the style but it was green, a dark green what they call Hunter green and a four door." Jeffrey looks over at the small bedside table where a carafe of water was sitting. Ron pours him a glass, handing it to him with a smile. "Thanks." Drinking the whole glass before handing it back. "I was starting to feel really lightheaded by then but

64

I remembered from some movie to count the turns so I counted, we were headed south when he pushed me in the car. We took two rights a left went straight for a while and then another left before we stopped. I heard a grinding noise and now I know it was a garage door sliding up, the car pulls in and stops. I don't know how long it was before he pulled me out but I know it wasn't right away. It was still daylight I could see the window in the garage but when he jerked me out the window was dark so I must have been left in the car the whole afternoon." He leans back against the pillows. "He pulled me to the other side of the garage where he tried to hook me up to some kind of chain pulley, but I fought back. Whatever he had given me was wearing off and I wasn't about to let him chain me up. Anyway I managed to land a few good punches when he pulled a knife out, we fought over that and I think he may have cut himself there a lot of blood dripping from him. I managed to kick the knife out of his hand and that's when he started punching me screaming that I was a present, that I was a gift." He snorts again. "Some gift. Anyway he landed a good punch to my head and I fell I remember hitting that hard concrete floor landing on some kind of piece of machinery I guess that's where I cracked my ribs. I got up he hit me in the head but this time I grabbed a wrench and hit him, I remember watching as he fell like in slow motion, he landed on his back and I could see his eyes, they were black, solid black and there was a scar slashing through his left eyebrow." He makes a slashing motion over his eye. "When he didn't move I hightailed it out of there. I know I made it to the corner before passing out then I woke up here."

I could tell the talk had taken it out of him so I stand. "Thank you Mr. Owens you've helped us a great deal. If we have any more questions for you we'll let you know."

He nods at us, barely able to keep his eyes open as we leave. The captain was waiting for us in the hallway. "Find out anything? Could this be our killer?"

I nod as I look to see who was within earshot. "Yes and I'd like to go to that warehouse and the sooner the better."

The captain nods as he writes the address down. "The crime scene techs are there now so you won't be alone." Ripping the sheet from his notebook he starts to hand it to me before holding it back a little. "Be careful and don't let Ron leave your side." He gives Ron a look which said leave her and you'll be back on patrol duty.

Making our way back to the parking lot before we say a word, as soon as we were clear the doors Ron grabs my arm making me stop in my tracks. "Sure you want to do this tonight?"

"Yes the sooner the better. Maybe I'll be able to sleep tonight."

With a groan and a loud mumble, we confiscate one of the patrol cars from an officer and head over to the warehouse district my mind racing with what we else we may find. This could be the lead we need.

Chapter 9

We reach the warehouse to find enough vehicles
to open a used car lot, but no Hunter green
Chevrolet in sight. Entering the bustling warehouse
I take in my surroundings as Ron talks to the
officer in charge.

The first thing I notice is the smell, this
wasn't an abandoned garage it was still in use. The
odor of grease, gasoline, oil and unwashed bodies
was too strong and fresh. Along with the puddles of
who knew what that were all over the floor.

Making my way carefully to where the halogen
lights were set up, I find a little hole in the
crowd to look at the scene of the fight, with
disappointment. The floor was still wet from
someone washing it, so our suspect was smart enough
to know to wash the blood away.

Walking around the garage trying to put myself
in Jeffrey's shoes as he was fighting. He mentioned
a window, there were several under the overhang
near the ceiling, all grimy and dusty. The

workbench was filled with tools of every description, used oily rags filled a box beside the bench. Tires were stacked against the wall with car parts stuffed in the center but above the tires on the wall was a crude drawing, very crude, to me it looked like a star. Calling a tech over I ask for pictures before motioning at Ron. When he was standing beside me. "What does that look like to you?"

Tilting his head sideways. "A star or a baseball diamond."

"What?" I look at the drawing again then pull the picture I had taken of the map up on my phone. "A diamond." That's what it was, a diamond. He told Jeffrey he was a present, a gift. All this is being done to impress someone. And that makes this person all the more dangerous because they weren't going to stop until they have who they were trying to impressed satisfied.

As Ron goes back to helping the techs I search further into the garage. I don't think this was used for any other victims and I had a feeling that he didn't work here maybe a friend or relative owned it. Making a note to ask Ron for a list of employees and the owner, I continue further into the garage to a back area that at one time may have been a storage room but was now just a collection spot for discarded car parts. Loose bolts and wires were scattered over the floor, empty oil cans and anti-freeze containers were tossed in the corner, broken steering wheels and cracked mirrors were in a pile, just trash but I continue looking anyway, you never know where you may find a clue.

Ending my search of the room I continue on until I come to the office. Staying by the door I take in the three desks that were pushed against the walls, all littered with yellowed paper, plastic bags, old fast food and candy bar wrappers along with ashtrays filled with cigarette butts. One wall had three file cabinets with none of the drawers shut, papers and files stuck out at all angles. The walls were covered with old calendars of motorcycles with the mandatory half naked woman sprawled on the seat, there were pictures of fast cars with women hanging out the windows, two posters of restored antique cars without a woman to make the car impressive and there was one picture of the garage probably taken decades ago with a man and two boys standing in front all with huge smiles, the sign hanging over the garage doors said 'Coleman Family Garage.' A family business that's time had come to an end.

Leaving the office door I study the layout of the garage one more time before walking out the garage doors. Standing back I look up to where the sign was, now a faded plank of wood that you could barely make out the words.

Leaning against a patrol car I take in the area, the presence of the police had undoubtedly disrupted work at the produce plant, trucks were loaded and waiting to leave, a couple were waiting down the street to unload and the men standing on the dock were casting very unpleasant glares at the officers.

At the other end of the street the yellow police tape was keeping back a slew of looky loos, many were taking pictures and videos, wonder what they think happened here?

One of the produce workers comes over to me. "Excuse me, can you tell me what's going on and when it's going to be done? We have produce to get out and some to be unloaded."

Turning to face the short, plump, grey haired man. "I'm sorry there was a crime committed there last night. They should be finished before long. I'm sorry for the inconvenience." Throwing his hands in the air along with a few choice words he turns back to yell at anyone who would listen about too many chiefs and not enough Indians.

A group of officers start coming from the building with Ron bringing the rear. Then the techs start loading their vans with their lights, boxes, and evidence bags. I turn back to see the short, plump, grey haired standing on the dock with his hands on his hips, a little grimace of a smile on his face.

"Ready?" Ron opens the driver's door to the cruiser, sliding in and starting the car before I have a chance to open my door. "Pick up anything?"

Shaking my head as a patrol officer rolls up the yellow tape letting us through, I was watching the crowd, the crowd that may have our culprit in their midst.

><

He got away. He got away. He'll go to the police and tell them. He needs to be stopped! Just kill him! He screams as he paces the floor. Kill him! The plans, the plans! He was supposed to be a present for my pretty now he's a vicious monster that needs to die! Ripping the bloodstained shirt off, he screams again. Kill him! The blood starts seeping from the knife wound again. The man stabbed me. Wrapping a bandage tightly around his arm. He's got to be killed.

><

Grace and Ron walk through the police station by the front door for a change, bypassing John Green's desk where he had the phone pressed to his ear giving them both glares as they pass. He was on desk duty now and apparently wasn't happy about it.

The captain was standing in front of his window when Grace sees him he motions for them to come inside. Once inside Grace takes the chair in front of his desk as Ron slouches on the couch. The captain sits behind his desk with his hands clasped together. "Well?"

Ron leans forward. "Unfortunately all the evidence seems to have been cleaned up, by water and oil, so anything that was left is contaminated. The techs went over everything, all the tools, the floor, the bay lift that Mr. Owens fell on. I don't think we'll find anything."

With a tight scowl on his face, the captain turns to me. "I didn't see anything other than a garage that's seen better days. The only thing I can think of is that Mr. Owens said he heard the garage door go up, so whoever this is had the remote. Maybe he works there or is related in some way. I noticed the garage was once Coleman and family, he could be part of the family to have access. Other than that, no I'm sorry."

The captain scrubs his face with his hands. "I was hoping he had made another mistake besides letting his victim go." Leaning forward again. "So what now?"

Ron and I look at each other before he answers. "Besides going through the names of the workers, I have no idea."

"We've walked through some of the neighborhoods where the victims lived. I'm not seeing that they were abducted from there. Tomorrow we'll walk through where they were found there has to be a connection somewhere." I see a little hope on the captain's face. "Any news on Mr. Owens?"

With a slight nod the captain fills us in. "He's been released with a squad sitting on him, but he said he was going to take a vacation. He's booked a flight for Florida, leaving tonight. Oh and the reason he wasn't incapacitated like the others, the doctors said he had enough caffeine in his system to start his own coffee shop."

Good to know, so whatever drug was being used caffeine diluted.

The captain stands. "Keep at it you two."

Being dismissed we head for my office. Unlocking the door we both collapse into chairs, Ron in front of my desk, me behind. "So now what?"

"For you sleep. Maybe food. For me, more digging."

"So no sleep for you?"

Stacking the files I stop, laying them back down. I was meticulous about the order I keep my files almost to the point of obsession. They weren't like I left them. I glance to the window that opens into the squad room to see John Green watching me. "Someone has been in my office. My files have been gone through." Thankfully the ones that had the ME's findings and my notes had been with me.

Ron stands up. "John."

I nod. "I would say so from the way he's watching us. I know there aren't any spare keys to this office, I made that request explicit. So did he pick the lock?"

Going to the door, Ron squats to look at the lock. John sees this and suddenly has a mission away from his desk. Turning back to me, Ron nods. "Several scratches on the lock and wood. May I suggest you don't leave anything here on the case."

"No need." Making sure John was still out of sight, I open the bottom cabinet door of the credenza behind my desk to reveal a safe.

"Whoa. Had no idea that was there. Don't trust much do you?"

"It isn't lack of trust, it's not wanting anyone to see my notes as I think a case through." Opening the safe, I slide the files and what I wasn't going to take home with me inside before shutting the door and closing the cabinet. "There, should be safe for tonight."

"And I'll get this locked changed." Holding a finger up. "With you having the only key."

"Thanks."

Tipping his head. "You are welcome. See you in the morning."

Giving him a smile goodbye as he shuts the door, I scan my desk to make sure I hadn't left anything out before turning off the lights and walking out. Heading for the front door I pass John. "Don't bother there aren't any files left in my office." Getting a death ray look in return, I left the precinct with a smile.

Chapter 10

Walking down the street I muse over why John Green was so interested in this case. Why was he making so many efforts to sabotage what we were doing? Leaking information to the press, telling the captain there were leads when there weren't, breaking into my office. Most detectives would be pleased to be off a case where there was no evidence, no leads, nothing except victims.

I never walk the same way home two days in a row, nor do I enter my apartment building by the same door every day. The building had three entrances, front, back and side. Today I was using the side entrance that was a block over from the front. Taking my time but noticing everything around me, the people, the cars, delivery vans, even the shops. Inserting my key into the side door, I push it open into a darkened hallway. Very few of the tenants use this so the lights were hardly ever on.

Climbing the stairs to the top floor, I hear the TV playing in my neighbor's apartment, normal. Unlocking my door, I go through my normal routine of setting everything down by the door and then checking the rest of the apartment. Compulsive? No. When you see what I've seen as a profiler and working with the police you know that people are capable of anything and the world was full of evil.

Finding nothing amiss, I shut and lock the door before kicking my shoes off and pulling my shirt loose. Setting my case on the coffee table, I head for my little kitchen and the coffee pot. After starting the coffee I wander to the bedroom to get some comfortable clothes on before I start my nightly marathon of trying to get into the mind of a killer.

Clicking the TV on, I flip until I find a silly movie leaving the volume low but loud enough to keep me company. Sitting down on the couch, I tuck my feet under me before pulling my hair back into a ponytail. Taking a sip of coffee I think of what the captain had said about the caffeine

79

diluting the drug that Mr. Owens had been given, we need to find out what that drug is.

Okay to work, opening my case I pull out my files and start reading…again, only this time I was concentrating more on the ME's reports. As I get into the first victim's file, I get the creepy feeling again. Rubbing my neck I glance at the window, was someone watching?

Getting up I walk to the window taking a good look at the building across from me. It was one floor shorter than this building but I couldn't see where anyone could look into my apartment from the top floor, but they could from the roof. Nothing was catching my attention so I pull the drapes resettling on the couch and continue reading.

><

She's home and looks so pretty with her hair like that. Her dark hair, hair that I can't wait to run my hands through. Her dark eyes, he can't wait to look into those eyes and see the pleasure of his gifts to her. He failed with the last one and now he sees that the police are protecting him, he has to be vigilant when he sees him again this time it won't be as nice as before this time it will be a knife across the throat. That way he'll be silenced for good. Watching his pretty as she watches TV, she's always reading, he hopes she enjoys it. Why is she closing the curtain! No! He can't see you when you do that! He screams. Why is everything getting so complicated? Pulling at his hair. He wants to watch her tonight! He needs to see her! His pretty- I can't see you! Screaming again, he slams open the roof door letting it crack against the wall, taking the stairs two at a time he descends until he's at the bottom and pushing open the door for outside. He looks back up at the window that his pretty was behind and screams again.

><

Tossing the file to the side just as my phone pings, looking at the text from the ME, 'we discovered each victim had a hank of hair cut from the back of their head'. Huh, interesting, he was taking a souvenir from each victim and probably after they were dead.

Closing my eyes, I lean my head against the back of the couch. I imagine myself in the place of one of the victims. Incapacitated. Drugged. Maybe alert enough to see my captor. Dark eyes boring into mine. The blade of a knife inches away from my face. The smell of the abandoned building filling my nostrils. The darkness overwhelming me. The pain. I jerk up, opening my eyes, sweat covering my face, cold chills running down my arms, my heartbeat racing.

Shaking the images from my head I pick up my coffee mug intending to fill it again but when I get to the kitchen I pull out the bottle of wine I had in the refrigerator. Filling a glass half full, I down it in one gulp.

Okay now that I officially had the sick psychopath in my head I needed to burn some energy. Looking at the clock, 10:30 pm, a little late to be taking a run through the streets of the factory district alone but if I run to the park I'll be joined by other late night runners.

Changing into long running shorts, I slip my shoulder holster on before tossing a sweatshirt over my head, slipping my feet into a pair of running shoes then tuck my weapon in the holster. Strapping my phone to my left arm and pepper spray to my right I was ready. Locking my door behind me I jog down the stairs and take the back door out of the building.

The park is three streets over so I take a direct route down an alley to reach Congress Boulevard and then cross over to District and the park. There were bright street lights every couple of yards so the park was illuminated enough that it felt like dusk instead of night.

Getting into my rhythm I let it take over, feeling the pounding of my feet hitting the pavement. Letting it sooth me. I start pushing a little harder passing other runners until I come to a well-toned man that seems to be as anxious as I was to release tension. He was dressed in black running shorts and a black tee shirt, his phone was strapped to his arm with ear buds attached. He was playing the music so loud I could hear it.

We were keeping pace with each other, each of us pounding on our demons with each footfall. Rounding the next bend we start up a slight incline before the path leads into a small grove of trees. Once we were under the cover of trees he grabs my arm pulling me to face him. I look into dark blue eyes, then at his dark hair that was pointing in every direction, he smiles just a little before leaning down, planting his lips on mine. I resist at first then wrap my arms around his neck. He pulls back. "Bad case?"

With my arms still wrapped around his neck, I bury my head in his chest. "Yes. How about you?"

Wrapping his arm around my shoulders as we start walking. "Quite a few concerned about the killings especially since there hasn't been much in the news about it." Lowering his head. "Anything you can tell me to ease some minds?"

"Sorry Wade but I can't discuss anything yet."

Nodding his understanding. "Will you be in service tomorrow?"

Smiling up at his chiseled face. "Of course." His dark eyes twinkle as they look at me. Wade

Caufrey, pastor of Concord Baptist Church, he was 40 years old, never been married and definitely one of the best looking guys I've ever seen. I couldn't say he was my boyfriend, I couldn't just say he was a friend, so I call him a possible. It's possible that one day he will be my boyfriend, it's possible we may take things further one day, it's possible we may decide to call whatever we have quits one day. It's all possible. But right now we see each other when we have time, we call when we can, we go out when we can, nothing serious.

"Race you back." For a pastor he gives me a mighty wicked grin before sprinting off.

"Hey no fair!" I take off at a fast clip to catch up to him just before he reaches the bend in the path.

Now that we were again running side by side, I start pushing myself a little harder, slowly passing him. Raising my arms in triumph as I pass him, I hear a chuckle then the pounding of feet as he catches up. We slow down to an easy jog, comfortable with each other and the pace we set.

Once we reach the end of the path and the entrance to the park, we stop. Bending over to catch my breath as Wade asks if I want to stop for a cup of coffee.

"Thank you. But now that my head is clearer I want to see if I can get some sleep." With the demons at bay for a little while, I need to at least try.

Taking my hand, he kisses my knuckles softly before leaning down to kiss me. "See you tomorrow then and try to leave a little time to have lunch with me after services are over. I miss you."

Returning his kiss, I pull away. "I will. Good night." With a wave over my shoulder I cross the street to take the alley back to my building. Entering through the back door I see the pulse of blue strobe lights reflecting on the hall walls. Looking out the front door, the street had several patrol cars parked at the curb with their lights on and several officers were talking to a cluster of people.

Not seeing anyone I know, I decide to not be nosy and head for the stairs and hopefully some sleep.

Chapter 11

Standing under the spray of water as hot as I can stand, I think of seeing Wade tonight. That definitely was the highlight of my day, maybe keeping him on my mind will chase the demon away for tonight.

Tossing on an over large tee shirt and baggy shorts I head for the kitchen, no more coffee but a little something on my stomach was a must. Clicking the TV on as I pass the first thing I hear is laughter, good that was just the background noise I needed to hear.

Fixing a light salad, carrying it and a glass of tea to the couch I settle into my little dent I've made over the years. My eyes settle on the TV and the show that was playing, it was an old episode of Friends and a classic.

Losing myself in the show, I finish my salad setting the bowl on the coffee table I lay down, tucking a pillow under my head before grabbing a light blanket off the back of the couch. My eyes close and welcome sleep comes.

Jerking awake it takes me a moment to realize I had fallen asleep on the couch, not the first time, won't be the last. Rubbing my face thinking back on the dreams that had tried to invade my sleep, my demon was taking shape now, and it wasn't good.

Pulling the drapes open to bright sunshine, it was going to be a nice day and I'd get to see Wade too, how good was that?

Starting a pot of coffee before getting ready for church, people were always surprised that I was a Christian, they couldn't wrap their mind around what I did for a living and believing in Jesus. To me it was a no brainer, look at Judas he was planning on killing Jesus so the bad guy has always been there since the beginning of time. I look at what I do as stopping the bad guy from hurting more people.

With my coffee in one hand and my mascara in the other I start getting ready, the one day a week that I actually take time with the way I look. Why?

Because there was always someone looking, always someone pondering what Wade would see in me instead of their granddaughter or daughter.

After tossing a simple black dress on, slipping my feet into black heels, I carry my mug to the kitchen for one last refill before leaving.

Sitting on the couch I reach across to straighten my piles of files up, a small piece of paper slips to the floor. It had been torn from a small notebook, one like most of the officers use, this one had three words on it, 'for my pretty.' Who's note was this? I knew it wasn't Ron's handwriting or the captain's for that matter. So who wrote it?

Knowing there wasn't much I could do about it now, I slip it into the top file then rinse my mug out before heading for church.

Leaving by the front door for a change I turn right to walk the eight blocks to the church. With a light step and a smile hoping that we could get together afterwards at least for lunch.

><

It's time to watch my pretty, he opens the ground floor door looking over his shoulder at her floor to see her curtains were open today then he stops, she was coming out the front door. He will follow her today. He will see where she goes. He'll stay on the opposite side of the street that way he can watch her face, her beautiful face, he can imagine her soft skin, her lips, her dark eyes smiling at him thanking him for all the presents he has for her. She stops on the corner looking behind her frowning. What was wrong? He looks around but doesn't see anything wrong. Maybe she hears something. No she keeps walking, wonder where we're going today? She stops at a large rock building, what is that? She walks to the front door and goes in. He walks to the front to see that it's a church. She's gone into a church!

He starts pulling at his hair. A church. Why would she go into a church? She has powers, she's protected, she doesn't need to go into such an evil place. A scream escapes him. He has to get her from the clutches of those people. But how?

People stare at him as they enter the building, don't they see the evil there? He screams again before he turns and runs. Run back to safety. Back to her shrine.

><

Stopping to speak to several people as I walk down the aisle to a pew close to the front with a good view of the pulpit, I survey the large crowd. When I first started attending this church you could almost count the people attending services on two hands. Now the sanctuary was almost full, good for Wade. He was an exceptional preacher, his sermons always seem to hit home.

Music starts playing in the background which is the signal that the service was getting ready to start. The choir starts filling the seats on the stage, then the music director comes out followed by Wade.

I smile when I see him, dressed in a beautifully cut black suit with a dark grey shirt and a bright red tie. His hair is ruffled as if he just ran his hands through it which he probably did. As he takes a seat on the pulpit he sees me and smiles. Returning his smile I hear someone clearing their throat, turning to my left I find Mrs. Finn shaking her head at me. She's always wanted her daughter and Wade to get together, but her daughter clearly didn't since she currently was dating a man that had more tattoos than skin and really liked the pierced look.

Closing my eyes I let go of the evil and let the peace of Jesus fill me, along with the songs. Listening to Wade preach on walking the right path in today's world I get immersed, completely forgetting what had been filling my mind for days. That's the power.

After the service was over I keep my seat as the people slowly file out with Wade and the Associate Pastor shaking their hands and wishing them a blessed week. Finally hearing the huge double doors click shut, I get up walking up the aisle to where Wade was waiting for me. "Really good sermon today."

He bows slightly. "Thank you." Looking at me with a smile. "And you look amazing." He kisses me on the cheek. "Care for lunch?"

Giving him a smile back. "That would be nice. Thank you." Tucking my hand in his elbow. "And where were you thinking of having lunch?" I knew that he had a weakness for the crabs caught around here and his favorite place was a little seafood shanty close to the pier.

Winking at me. "Guess."

"The Crab Shack."

"You know me well." Holding the door for me we walk out into the bright sunshine.

We take our time walking to the pier, enjoying the day and the time with each other. Catching up on our lives when Wade asks. "How's the case? I know you can't tell me anything but from what I've heard so far this is a nasty one."

"It is. Gruesome and the demon taking residence. I have a feeling this one is going to play out badly."

"No clues yet huh?"

"Not a one."

94

Reaching the shanty, the aroma of spicy shrimp, buttered lobster and fried potatoes fills the air. My stomach rumbles a little as we choose a table next to the dock, telling the waiter what we want since we both knew the menu by heart. The light breeze fills my nostrils with the scent of the bay while it lightly ruffles my hair. I feel Wade tuck a loose strand behind my ear.

Chapter 12

><

Getting anxious as he waits for the people to come out of that evil place, he pulls his hair. Where is she? The doors open. There she is, my pretty. But what is she doing? She's letting another touch her! She's letting him lead her away! She's going with him! He screams. She can't be with another! He needs to follow them. He needs to see. He needs to see their faces. He needs to see. He screams as a bus blocks his way. He screams when the bus moves and they're gone. He's kidnapped her! My pretty! He screams.

><

While I'm enjoying my shrimp scampi and Wade is devouring crabs like they were the last on earth I see Ron sitting at the bar enjoying his own seafood meal. I nod in his direction, when Wade turns to see who I was talking about he gives me a nod.

Pushing my chair back, I walk to the bar standing behind Ron I lean close to his ear. "Good lobster?" I ask a little loudly which makes him jump to my heart's delight.

"Grace! Why don't you scare a person to death? Jeez." Wiping his mouth I get a really nasty look.

"It was just too tempting. Have you been in yet?" I was planning to go in after lunch.

"Not yet. Been to two complaints about some crazy guy screaming his head off." He points a finger at me as he takes another bite. "One was across the street from your building. Heard any screaming lately?"

"No but that explains the police presence there yesterday." Interesting. I give him a wave goodbye as I rejoin Wade.

He was paying the bill as I sit down. With a little smile he says. "Ready?"

I nod as he holds my chair. We walk slowly back to the church making tentative plans to try to meet during the week.

Chapter 13

After leaving Wade, I walk back to my apartment to change clothes before heading to the courthouse. As I approach the front door the creepy feeling comes over me. Looking around as I rub my neck, nothing seems out of the ordinary. I wave at Jed who owns the store across the street before going inside.

Inside I do my usual check before shutting and locking the door. As I start to pull my dress off, something makes me close the drapes first. I stop. Did I just see someone on the roof across the street? Sliding the drapes open again I study the rooftop but don't see anything. Pulling them shut again I decide that this case was making me paranoid.

Changing into my usual work attire I start to pack the files up then stop. We were going to check out the locations where the victims were found so I really didn't need them. Stuffing my pockets with what I'd need, I leave the building by the side door for the four block walk to work.

><

Oh my pretty is home, he watches as that evil man left her to walk home alone. He would take care of him. For putting his vile hands on her skin. He watches her. She looks so pretty today. But no! She shuts the curtains again! Why? Why won't you let him look at you? Why won't you let him watch you? Why? He screams as he leaves the roof. Why?

><

Entering the courthouse through the side door then letting myself into the police station, I notice how quiet it was compared to the other day. Checking the desks in front before going to my office I don't see John Green manning the phones today. Maybe they took pity on him and let him have a day off.

Reaching my office to see the new lock with a note taped to the window, 'check the diamond.' Huh. Going into the old conference room that Ron and I had been using, I walk to the map, studying it for a minute before I smile. "Clever." Turning back around to face the white board lifting the picture of Andrea to find my new office key taped to the board. "Yes you are clever Ron." Pulling the key loose before picking a pencil up and erasing the tiny drawing of a key from the map at Andrea's address.

With a smile I return to my office to find Ron leaning on the wall. Holding the key up. "That was good."

He bows. "Thank you. I tied to think of a way to hide it without anyone finding it."

"Has anyone ever told you that you would make a great detective?" Pushing the door open the first thing I think of is coffee so I pick up the coffee pot only to have a cup magically appear in front of my face. "Wow. You are really batting a thousand today."

With a slight bow. "Thank you. But I thought we'd want to get right out there today."

Looking at Ron's face. "You have something?"

"No, no. Just want to get this wrapped up."

"Ah. Nightmares?"

"Yes. How do you do this? Get in their heads? They take over." I could see the ghost of fear in his eyes.

"Yes they do. They slowly take over until you really start to think like them. But. When they're caught, the demon leaves and you have a feeling of euphoria that is almost unexplainable."

Ron nods as he takes a sip of coffee. "If you say so." Looking around. "Do we need to go over anything else?"

"No. Let's go." Locking the door behind us, tossing the key in the air before pocketing it. "Brilliant." We leave by the front door. Pulling my sunglasses down over my eyes I ask. "Walk or drive?"

"Walk."

Pulling a list from my pocket. "Let's start at the closest which will be the old ball field at the park."

Nodding as he finishes off his coffee tossing the cup in a trash can. Putting his own sunglasses on as we wait for a traffic light to cross the street. "I know that this is what you do, getting in the killers head, but I don't understand how. I mean all we know is his way of killing, we don't know him or who."

I wait until there weren't as many people around us. "It's hard to explain. I start with the victims, learning their lives, the way they live. That's what we did the other day. So I put myself in their shoes more or less. I live their lives for a day or so then start on the ME's reports, the way they were found, the way they were killed, how they were killed, if there was anything left behind or trophies taken. I mentally walk through each victim's death and that's when the demon comes into my head and starts to take over. I got a text from doc, he said a hunk of hair was cut from the back of each victims head, so there's the trophy."

"Hum. Each victim was dark haired with dark eyes." Glancing over at him I could tell he was taking in the dark haired, dark eyes people that you pass in a single day.

Reaching the street the park was on the people parade slows down to passing another person every five minutes instead of five seconds. Fewer stores but more homes start to line the street, then they stop until you were in the open with nothing on either side but empty lots. The park hasn't been used in years except for the neighborhood kids playing ball and they've made a good dirt path to follow. Reaching the field, I stop. The white markings of the baseball diamond were long gone, but the dirt tracks were still there. The victim had been found in the middle on the pitcher's mound. As Ron walks to the mound I take in the area.

At night no one would know anyone would be out here. No streetlights, no lights from homes, no lights from businesses it would be total darkness.

There had been no drag marks or tire tracks found, but the ground was hard enough that tracks probably wouldn't have been left anyway. Slowly I walk to the pitcher's mound, no trail of blood was found so that meant the victim had been dead for a while before being brought here. Circling the mound picturing the way they were found. This was where Robert Glesson had been found. Beaten, bruised, stabbed twelve times in the abdomen, chest and neck, one broken hand, and a hank of hair cut off. Still walking slowly around the mound then I move a little further away, I keep this up until I'm back to the outside of the diamond. That's when I see it. Squatting I study the tooth as Ron walks up, squatting beside me.

"You think that belongs to the killer?"

"Good possibility. It isn't that old and none of the victims were missing any teeth." Ron hands me a plastic baggie which I put the tooth in. Holding it up, "There's no blood on it but it belongs to a grown up." Pocketing the tooth I continue walking around the field but not finding anything else except trash.

Meeting back with Ron at the edge of the field. "So what's your take in this?" He was really trying to understand how I put the puzzle pieces together.

"Nothing really. Although if that tooth happens to belong to the killer. We may get lucky on DNA if he's in the system, or better yet check with a few dentists around here to see if any of their patients have come in with missing teeth." I immediately think of Dr. Shaw, he was my dentist and he loves a good mystery, he may be able to help.

Making our way to the piers, we head north to the park above the post office. This park was well kept and active being that is was close to the piers, the farmers market and quite a few businesses. Entering through the wide black wrought iron gates I pull my list out telling Ron that the victim was found within the perimeter of the fountain. The empty fountain that the city had been working on.

Thankfully the area around the fountain was clear of people, maybe because of the construction equipment scattered around. There was still yellow crime scene tape around the fountain so that was probably keeping people with kids away.

Walking around the fountain, I check my notes on how the victim was found. In the middle with her hands behind her head, her legs crossed at the ankles. She had been stabbed twelve times in the abdomen and sides, she had two broken ribs, her face had multiple bruises along with a broken jaw, her knuckles were scraped and bruised, good maybe she was able to get a few punches in. Stepping into the empty fountain to where the body was placed trying to get a feeling on why here.

Ron was standing on the lip of the fountain. "The diamond."

"What?"

"The diamond shape." He motions with his hands the rim of the fountain. "The map. The paint you found in the garage, the baseball diamond. The fountain is shaped like a diamond."

I get up on the rim of the fountain, and yes it was shaped like a diamond. Something Mr. Owens said came back to me. "He said 'my pretty' to Mr. Owens, so is he doing this for his girlfriend or for his conquest?"

"Huh?"

"There's someone he's trying to impress. A woman, his pretty. He's doing this as a gift for her in his delusional way of thinking. This guy isn't into any kind of cult or wiccan, he's just plain crazy."

Jumping off the fountain rim Ron says. "Hell of a way to get someone's attention and by the way, it that the correct term to use, crazy?"

"No but it fits." I walk around the fountain with not much hope of finding anything since besides the police the construction workers had been here. "Okay next one is actually in a building at the dock, another on the pier."

Chapter 14

We stop at a local diner before heading to the dock. I ordered a hamburger with fries while Ron ordered a hoagie. As we ate he kept shaking his head until I couldn't take it anymore. "What?"

Raising his eyebrows at me. "Huh?"

"You keep shaking your head what are you thinking?"

Wiping his mouth, he places both arms on the table leaning forward. "So you want a girl's attention, you think this may be the girl of your dreams. You think she's pretty and want to get her gifts. So why people? What kind of gift is a dead person and to top it off he's not giving them to her, the only way she would know is if he took pictures or she read the papers. So how's that a gift?"

I knew he was trying to wrap his head around this but trying to understand a person that wasn't in their right mind was almost impossible. "I know in your mind a gift means going to the store and buying your girlfriend a gift, maybe a piece of jewelry or a book by her favorite author. But he doesn't think that way. He sees a human body as the ultimate gift, a sacrifice, an offering and placing it in a diamond to him means undying love as if he was placing that diamond on her finger. What I'm not understanding is the boy girl pattern he's started. To me I could understand all men because that way he would be showing her he was getting rid of competition or symbolizing slaves to her. But the women to me would seem like it would represent others wanting his love and therefore competition for her love, which she isn't even aware of yet."

Ron's eyes get big. "You mean that his pretty isn't even aware what he's doing?"

"I'd say probably not. Not that I'm saying she's normal but if he was in a relationship meaning he was already with her, I would see them both doing the killing and one of them would have made a mistake by now. So this woman he's fixated on isn't aware these brutal killings are for her and once she does find out will reject him totally and he'll go off the rails completely."

"So besides just having a serial killer we may wind up with someone just killing to be killing and at random?" His face blanches a little. "Wonder if it's too late to ask the captain to reassign me."

"Too late for that now, you're in too deep." Reaching over I take his hand. "Trust me once we have him the demons will leave and you'll treat it like a homicide as always."

Taking a deep breath. "I sure hope you're right."

"Let's go check out these two then call it a day. May I suggest an overload of sugar tonight and the dumbest thing you can find on TV." After we take care of the tab, I pull my list out. "Okay the next one is on Pier 10 at the equipment shed."

"This ought to be good, how can there be a diamond where heavy duty equipment is kept?"

"Good question." We walk in silence until we find the shed with a piece of yellow crime tape fluttering on the side. Looking around the deserted pier thinking what a shame that most of the piers had shut down because of the economy. We take the time to check the area around the shed looking for any clues or disturbances, but there was nothing, of course it's been a couple of weeks now so any physical evidence would of course be gone.

Standing in front of the massive double doors that open the shed, Ron starts pushing one side open while I try to open the other side, unfortunately it was too heavy and I couldn't budge it. Waiting as Ron gets both sides open before looking inside.

The massive shed was dark with no windows and the only entrance was the two doors. Ron flips the overhead fluorescent lights on which immediately flood the shed with bright light. Besides the walls fully lined with shelves filled with every imaginable kind of tool, part, cans, tires and several things I had no idea what they were, there were five huge machines lined up neatly.

Retrieving my notes, the body was found on the front of the loader, whatever the heck that was. "Do you have any idea what a loader is?"

I get that typical man look of you've got to be kidding me. With a slight smile he points to the largest machine that was sitting right in front of me, of course.

Studying the gigantic beast then looking at my notes on how the body was placed. Walking around the machine I find what I was looking for on the back. A large fluorescent orange sign attached to the back of the machine and with a tiny stretch of the imagination it looks like a diamond. The chains that held the victim are still attached to the machine, but nothing else to even indicate a body had been strapped to the machine. Walking around the machine, looking at all the parts to the thing, leaning down I look underneath then drop to my knees. Reaching as far as I can I finally manage to grab the small slip of paper. Scooting back out from under the loader I look at the paper, it's a torn piece from a movie poster, an old movie poster.

"Ron look at this." He comes across the room from where he was looking at the other machines. "This was under the loader. Now my way of thinking this is a poster from an Indiana Jones movie that was out in the 80's if I remember correctly so why would it be in a place that's used daily? This must have come from an abandoned theatre. So we need to find where that would be and how many there are."

With a smile he pulls out his phone. "I can only think of two, one near the harbor and the other close to your building." He starts swiping at the screen on his phone. "Yep only two left. So no more looking at locations of where the body was found?"

"No, I don't think so. But it's starting to get dark so let's pick up tomorrow." We start walking toward the street.

"Sounds good to me. Want to get a cab back?"

Thinking of how far away we were from my building I decide to walk it instead. "No thanks I'll walk. I want to stop and pick up something for dinner later."

"Careful Grace."

Thanking him as he hails a cab, I let the poster consume my thoughts as I walk toward home.

><

This is all his fault. He made me do this. He drove me to this. He touched my pretty, he laid his hand on her, he defiled her! Watching as the woman walks toward me just like everyone else looking at her phone. As she gets close enough he steps out, wrapping his arm around her neck as he pulls her into the doorway. Slamming the door behind him, he tosses her to the ground, she hits her head and is quiet. Good that will give him time to tie her so she can watch as he sacrifices her for my pretty. He pulls the zip tie tight around her ankles so she can't kick him like that cretin did and he lost a tooth. This time he'll make sure she can't get loose like the last guy did and goes to the cops. After he finishes tying her he stuffs a rag in her mouth, he can't take the chance that she'll scream. It's a shame she doesn't have dark hair like my pretty it would be a better sacrifice if she did. Pulling her hair away from her face he sees her eyes are open and they're blue, no this can't be! Taking his knife he stabs and stabs and stabs her until he can't anymore. This is an abomination! He can't use her as a gift, he can't let my pretty

know he's killed someone not worthy of her!

Spitting on the woman as contempt fills him, he

leaves letting her lie in her blood to rot.

Chapter 15

Stopping at the corner market, I pick up some vegetables for a salad and some fresh shrimp to make scampi for dinner. Grabbing another container of coffee and just for fun a gallon of double chocolate ice cream, it may be a long night.

Carrying my purchases home a man runs out of the building I was walking beside, almost knocking me down. Staring after him I wonder what his big hurry is before mentally shaking my head and continuing on to cross the street to my building. Entering by the front door, I take the stairs to my floor, hearing the TV in the apartment next door I drop my bag before unlocking the door and doing my ritual of checking the apartment out before locking myself in for the night.

Stowing the groceries away before turning the TV on, I take a chance and open my drapes for the last of the afternoon sun to come in. Gazing at the building across from me, not seeing anything unusual or getting that creepy feeling, I head for my bedroom to change clothes.

My phone dings as I head back to the kitchen to fix myself supper, looking at the display I smile, it was from Wade. 'Just a thank you for today, we need to do that more often.' I text back that I agree. With a smile I prepare a large salad as the shrimp scampi cooks in the oven. Pulling a loaf of garlic bread from the freezer, I toss that in the oven before finishing the dressing for my salad.

Dropping some ice in a glass then filling it with tea, I take my glass and a pile of napkins along with my salad to the living room placing everything on the coffee table before grabbing the shrimp and bread from the oven. Oh this smells so good!

As I enjoy my dinner, I watch a rerun of an old Doris Day movie, just what I need to get my mind clear. After the movie finishes, I clean my mess up before getting back into the files.

Closing the drapes as I settle back down, feeling better that no one can see me. Why was I having these creepy feelings that I thought someone was watching me. That's never happened before as I work on a case. Shaking my head of that thought I open my laptop. Taking the photo of each victim I line them up side by side then study the pictures.

The men all had short dark hair that had that ruffled look, like they're fingers are a comb. Their faces were all nicely shaped except for one that's cheeks were a little fuller than the others. The women all have dark unruly hair and their faces are well shaped. I take the women's pictures overlaying them on top of each other, definitely close, same with the men when I overlay their pictures. With the shapes of their faces they could be related.

So he was choosing his victims carefully, very carefully. Was he watching them from one certain place? What was the connection? None of the victims had anything in common except a couple liked to play a video game called Game of Conquest.

Deciding I needed to check that out, I find the game but the cost to download was ridiculous. Knowing there was an electronics store on the next block, I call them asking if they by chance have the game and what I get was, 'go online and download it', sheesh. No I wasn't doing that. Instead I pull some sneakers on, grab my keys and wallet and a light jacket before leaving to head for the closet coffee shop that had Wi-Fi access.

Entering the busy coffee shop I get in line for a large cup of regular before scanning the room. In the corner was a large table that held three young men. All bent over their laptops, with headphones on, two were grinning from ear to ear the other looked as if he was getting his butt royally kicked.

Taking a chance I walk behind them looking at the computer screens, they were definitely playing games. The boy I was standing behind just killed four men and was now fighting a huge monster of some kind, a cross between a dragon and a transformer. What was this stuff?

Feeling eyes on me I raise mine to find the unhappy kid staring at me, taking one side of his earphones off. "Something wrong lady?"

Giving him a smile. "Is this Game of Conquest?"

He guffaws. "No way." Motioning with his head for me to come around the table. "This is Game of Conquest."

Okay, this was set two thousand years ago, something called the Black Watch was after people that wanted to get on the other side of the wall, whatever that was. "Can you play a little for me?"

"Sure." He starts the game which is set in snow covered mountains, with a hooded figure hunting a man. He walks me through the scene until the man shoots the other with a crossbow. But as soon as he does other hooded figures appear from the woods. The boy takes me through several levels of the game until he's gotten all of the hooded figures. "Now I have to get closer to the wall before more knights come. Then I have to get rid of them."

With a basic understanding I thank the boy before asking what they had been drinking. Asking the barista to refill their drinks, paying for them and leaving her a tip as I walk from the coffee shop. Now I had another clue, maybe this explains the use of a knife instead of a gun.

A light rain has started falling so I double time it back to my building. Taking the stairs two at a time, I open my door to see everything just as I had left it. TV on, papers scattered over the coffee table and couch. Locking the door behind me, I hang my damp coat up and kicking my shoes off as I walk to the couch.

The boy at the coffee shop said you could play the game on a computer or TV so I'm thinking they all had the game we were just concentrating on the computers. Sending an email to our IT guy at the station I ask him to check the TV's of the victims for the game. If this was the link between them all, then maybe there was a group that met or conversed about the game, something like the Comic Con's that were all over the place now.

While I wait for an answer from my email, I play with the pictures some. For fun I pull a picture of myself up, overlaying it with the others, wow, really close except I have light green eyes instead of dark brown. I close my eyes, in the game everyone had dark hair and eyes. And a gift was a death.

My heartbeat increases a little with each find, I knew I was on the right track. Now to find if there was a group that met. Going back to my browser I Google Game of Conquest, then groups, then meetings, then conventions, but get nothing. I should have asked that boy at the coffee shop about it. No I need to ask our IT guy, the man knew everything about gaming, he had been in some competition over a war game not long ago and came in third. So tomorrow I needed to spend some time with him.

Feeling like I had made some progress today, the demons were laying quiet and while they were I decide to indulge in a little ice cream and try for some sleep.

Chapter 16

Waking the next morning to a grey sky with the weatherman saying periods of heavy rain, I groan. It wasn't that I hated the rain I just didn't like walking to work in it. After two large mugs of coffee I get dressed in layers in case we did have to go out today. Packing my case with all the files I had, tucking other necessities in my pockets I lock the door and head downstairs taking the front entrance today.

Pulling my hood up and keeping my head down I quick walk the four blocks to the office and still managed to get soaked with the wind blowing rain in my face. Running up the front steps I pull the door open to run smack dab into John Green.

"Watch it!" He snarls at me.

"Me. What is your hurry?" I wasn't in the mood to butt heads with him today. Without answering he stomps past me.

Muttering to myself as I shake my coat to get the excess water off before entering the station to see a typical Monday morning. Little clusters of officers going over the weekend's calls, what needed to be handled today, Sheila manning the phones with a smile and a nod at me. And thank you that Ron was making a fresh pot of coffee.

Saying hello as I walk to my office, I hang my coat up before tossing my bag on the desk then smile at the mug of coffee that appears. "Thank you."

Ron nods at me. "You're welcome. We may need a couple of pots today what with the weather." He stares at me for a minute. "What's up?"

I must have a really big smile on my face. "I think I figured a few things out." Plopping down in my chair. "But I'm afraid we may have to talk to the IT guy."

Ron pulls the chair in front of my desk to where he can put his feet up. "Why's that?"

Running through everything I learned last night and my thoughts on it I can see his mind working before he smiles. "I know just the guy to talk to." Standing up. "Come on let's go."

"Go where?" Grabbing my wet coat off the hook. "I was only going downstairs to the IT department."

"I know someone better." He signs a car out then we take the elevator to the garage level.

As I get in the passenger seat. "Who's better than the IT guy?"

With a big smile he answers. "You'll see."

"Okay leave me in the dark."

Chuckling he guides the car to the expressway, where was he going? Keeping my mouth shut as he drives, I impatiently tap the armrest as we head west of Boston. Weaving his way off the expressway then through residential streets until he stops in front of a rambling one story brick house. "We're here." He jumps from the car waiting for me to join him on the porch.

As I reach him he opens the door yelling. "Mom! You home?"

His mother? She was the guru that could figure out games? No way.

"Ronnie? What are you doing here? Shouldn't you be at work?" A short dark haired woman with bright blue eyes meets us in the hallway wiping her hands on a towel. She reaches up, grabbing Ron by his ears before pulling his face down to give him a kiss.

"Hey mom. We are working. This is Grace Hanson, Grace my mom Ellen."

Holding my hand out. "Pleased to meet you."

"You too dear. Now what brings you here? Am I in trouble?" Ellen quirks an eyebrow at Ron.

"No, I just need to talk to Joey. Is he home?"

Waving her hand. "He's always home. Cant's blast that boy out of the basement." She points to a closed door in the hallway. "I'll fix some coffee while you find your brother."

His brother! Following Ron as he runs down the carpeted steps that led to the basement or should I say huge rec room. There were enough boy toys down here to keep ten men happy for the rest of their lives. As I follow Ron, I pass two bedrooms and a huge bathroom before we enter another large room full of computers, monitors, speakers and one gigantic TV. This was a computer geek's dream.

A man was sitting in front of a massive monitor that had cryptic words scrolling across the screen. He seems oblivious that we were even in the room.

Ron claps the man on the back. "Hey man, how you doing?"

The chair swings around to reveal a man with a younger model of Ron's face but he was slim with longer hair. "Ron, bro!" He gets up to reveal that he was at least two inches taller than Ron. As the two brothers hug I watch the computer monitor finally figuring out that he was hacking because the screen was now flashing 'access granted.'

"Joey this is Grace, she works with me and we need some help if you don't mind."

Ron tilts his head toward me which I take was my cue to smile and say. "Pleased to meet you."

"Whoa bro. Sure it's just work?" He wiggles his eyebrows before he turns to me. "Nice to meet you and I'm sorry you have to work with this jerk."

"Yeah it's a challenge some days." I nod at the screen. "Seems to be waiting for you."

Turning back to the computer he sits down, his fingers running over the keyboard faster than I could keep track. "I have a client that keeps getting hacked and I just found out why. Going to cost him some big bucks to get this problem fixed." He opens an email quickly typing a message before the turns back to us. "Now what kind of help do you need?"

Ron pulls another desk chair over before motioning for me to do the same. Grabbing the other chair, I pull it close. Once I was seated Ron starts to explain what Joey does for a living. "Grace, Joey is a genius when it comes to anything electronic. He can hack, he can trace a hacker, he can destroy any game made and he makes a pretty good living at it." Glancing at Joey I see his cheeks turning a little pink. Ron continues talking. "Joey we're working on a case where all the victims appear to be into Game of Conquest pretty heavy. We need to know if there's a group or club for these guys and also if there's a connection."

Joey steeples his fingers together. "Does this have anything to do with those six murders?"

Turning my eyes to Ron. "Yes it does. Do you think you can help us some?"

Staring at his brother with a frown, I was waiting for a no to come out of his mouth but then his face lights up with a huge smile. "You bet." Rubbing his hands together. "What's first?"

I speak up. "First I'd like to know if there is a club or group for these people."

"These people? You mean gamers? Yes there's several." Turning to his keyboard, he types for a second before he points to the screen which shows a satellite view of Court Street in Boston which is close to the piers. Pointing to a large building that appears to be painted solid black. "This building is divided into what is called piers. Each floor has two sections for specific games. Usually the most popular is on the ground floor. But Game of Conquest has been around a few years and has a massive following so the entire second floor is dedicated to them. They have the place decorated like the game even the wait staff dresses in hoods with black cloaks." He leans back. "Are you thinking of going in? Cause I can tell you now neither one of you would fit."

"I've seen a demonstration of the game but it was quick, can you walk us through it?"

He nods as he swivels his chair to a different computer, this one with a huge monitor. With a few clicks the screen pops to life filling it with images of men clashing their swords together in battle. Joey clicks on new player. "I'm past all the levels the game has so we'll create a new player to start at the beginning." He types in Grace as the new player then clicks play. As he maneuvers through the scene he narrates what he's doing and why, who he has to kill to get through to the next level and the reason that all of the characters have names like Lord Mox. After playing through three levels he turns to me. "Have an idea of what's going on now?"

I nod my head because I did have a general idea but not a clear one.

"Okay so let's get online now and get with some other players." Going back to the beginning screen he clicks on another button for internet play. A second later he's in the middle of a battle with dozens of others but this time some of the characters in the game look different.

"Why do these look different?"

"Good eye. Before we were just playing the game as it was written but now we're on with other players and they've created their own avatars or villains." He points to the screen to an evil looking character named Zantol. "That's me. Now watch."

I watch as he crushes his opponents with one slash of his sword, stomps on others that were lying on the ground then raises his sword in triumph pointing it to the wall that was in the background where a figure dressed in white was standing. Pointing to the figure Joey explains. "That's the conquest, her freedom from the capture of the North."

"Can you get closer to her?" My stomach does a little dance when Joey zooms in on her, not from hunger but the figure was a woman with long dark hair with dark eyes. My pretty.

My face must have shown my joy because Ron asks. "What?"

Pushing my chair back so he can get a better view. "Look at her, what do you see?"

Ron studies the image for a minute then smiles. "The prize, my pretty."

Nodding at him while Joey looks to us in confusion. We explain that the culprit called his victims gifts for his pretty, his unrequited love.

Joey's eyes get big before he turns back to the screen. He changes players back to his name then moves to level 200, the screen opens to find Joey's character holding onto the woman figure in celebration of winning her, the sound changes from music to an electronic voice that says, 'I have won you my pretty to be mine forever.'

Total silence fills the room. Joey clears his throat. "So you're thinking this guy is playing the game in real life?"

"Kind of sounds like it doesn't it." Ron rubs his face with his hands.

Leaning forward I ask. "Joey this building you mentioned, you've been there before?"

With a nod. "Yes several times but I was kind of asked not to come back."

"Why is that bro, because you beat everyone else?"

"Yeah. I did." He sits up straighter. "But I can go back in, probably won't be able to play but I can go in. Want me to stake the place out?"

Ron slaps his brother on the back. "Not without us."

"Come on you two will stand out like an elephant in the ballet. No way." A pinging noise made all three of us jump, Joey slides over to another computer monitor looking at the screen before smiling. "Ah seems as if your IT guy is asking for some help." He taps a few keys. "Huh he wants me to come to the station to go with him and check out some of the electronics that were found. Care to give me a lift?"

I remembered that I had emailed Greg with a thought, he must have followed up on it.

"Why would our IT guy want to talk to you?" Ron looks over at me.

"I emailed him last night on my thoughts, but the real question is how does he know your brother?"

Joey stands up sliding a shirt on. "Oh he doesn't know I'm Ron's brother, he knows me from ZoneRoom and of course from my skills he knows I'm a much superior IT man than he is." With a smug look on his face, he gets out of the reach of Ron. Following him up the stairs as he screams for his mom.

"Lord have mercy Joey, I'm not deaf I can hear you clump up the stairs." Her hands go to her hips. "Now what do you want?"

"I'm going out for a while with Ron." He leans over to give his mother a kiss. "Don't wait up for me." Joey heads for the front door leaving me and Ron.

Shaking his head Ron leans over to kiss his mother. "Sorry mom, I'll make sure he gets home."

Wrapping her arms tight around Ron's waist. "No thank you son for getting that boy out of the house for a while. Keep him as long as you want."

Thanking her I follow Ron from the house to find Joey sitting in the driver's seat. "Keys bro?"

"Oh get your butt over you've never driven a car in your life."

Once the boys were settled in the front seat I ask Ron. "Mind dropping me off at the dentist?"

"Sure where is it?"

"On District. Just drop me at the corner."

The boys bicker back and forth the whole way back to town. Even with the age difference you could tell they had a special relationship which was nice.

Chapter 17

Dropping me on the corner, I wave as the boys drive off hoping that Joey will be able to figure out if all the victims were Game of Conquests addicts. I turn to the large brick building on the corner, entering through the double glass doors then taking the elevator to the fifth floor where Dr. Shaw's office was, hoping that he wasn't swamped with patients.

Pushing the office door open to find an empty waiting room I walk over to the receptionist, Michelle. "Hi Michelle."

With a bright smile she greets me. "Grace how are you? Are you having a problem with a tooth?"

"No everything's fine. I was wondering if I could talk to Dr. Shaw for a minute."

Michelle leans closer and whispers. "Is this about a case?" Everyone in the office thinks that I'm a detective.

"Yes it is in a way." I smile at her hopefully to set her mind at ease.

Giving me a wink she picks the phone up asking for Dr. Shaw to come to the waiting room. By the time she had the phone back in the cradle Dr. Shaw was entering the room. Of medium height, trim, you could tell he worked out with short dark hair and sparkling dark brown eyes. "Grace. Good to see you. How can I help you?" Shaking my hand as he asks.

"Dr. Shaw. I was wondering if you could help me with a couple of questions." Pulling the plastic bag from my pocket. "We found this at a scene and was wondering if you have any idea how long it's been, well, out of the mouth and whether it's from a man or woman."

Dr. Shaw smiles at me before saying. "You realize I can't give any information out if it is a patient right?"

I nod my understanding. "Of course. Right now I'm more interested in how long it's been out and whether you can tell what gender and maybe age of the person." I scrunch my forehead up in hopes of a positive answer.

Laughing at my face. "Sure come on let's see what we have."

Following him to a small room that appears to be a lab of some sort where Joyce was cleaning her coffee mug. "Hello Grace, must be serious if he's bringing you in the lab." She leaves with a smile and a pat on my back.

Watching as he pulls a pair of gloves on before opening the plastic bag, extracting the tooth. Looking at it through a small eye magnifier he says. "Young probably. Looks to be fairly fresh. Whoever it is took care of their teeth." Raising the eye magnifier away he places the tooth in something that looks like a microscope. Turning a few knobs. "I'd say male from the length but we'll make sure. Maybe out of the gum ten days. And since the root is intact I would say they took a good punch directly in the mouth, this is a canine tooth." He points to the front of his own teeth, tapping on a tooth beside his front ones. "Now let's see if it's make or female." His hands move fast as he rubs the tooth with a tiny cloth. "Male."

Leaning on the counter. "DNA?"

With his bright smile. "Ah you want all the answers today." Placing the tooth on a tray he pulls a drawer open to expose dental tools of all varieties. My teeth clinch at the sight. Scraping a little at the root of the tooth letting the dust fall into a small glass container, putting the lid on, he tucks the tooth back into the plastic bag returning it to me. "This is about the serial killer isn't it? His face was somber looking now which wasn't a good look for him.

"Yes. I found this at one of the scenes where a victim was found. I'm hoping to get something to either narrow our search down or tell us who it is."

Getting up from the stool he had been sitting on he tucks an arm through mine. "Anything I can do to help. But you realize this isn't TV, I can't have DNA for several days maybe a week."

"Thank you Dr. Shaw."

As I reach the door. "Oh Grace. How long has it been since you've had a checkup?"

With my hand on the doorknob ready to make my escape. "Um, it hasn't been that long."

I open the door as Michelle calls out. "It's been eight months Grace. I can make an appointment for next Tuesday at 1 pm. Is that okay?"

Knowing I was caught I turn to look at Dr. Shaw who had his hand over his mouth to hide a huge smile. "Fine Michelle. Are you happy now Dr. Shaw?'

"Immensely."

As I leave the two to enjoy my misery, my phone rings. It was Ron. "Hey Ron, have you two found anything out?"

Ron's voice was excited. "All of the victims were heavily into Game of Conquest. The ones that we couldn't find a computer had it on their TV's. Joey says that each one was past the two hundredth level, so they were all experts at the game."

"Good we have a connection now. So when do we go to the ZoneRoom?"

"That's the other good news. There's a tournament tonight."

I could hear Joey in the background saying we both needed to geek up.

"I assume you heard that?"

"Yes and what does he mean by geek up, we look like every other millennial on town." By that I meant we both dressed like every other thirty year old in town.

"Wait he's showing me pictures of the last competition and whoa, we need to geek up. I'll send you some of these photos to show you. I'll pick you up at 7 pm okay?" As I end the call my phone pings, pulling the photos up. "Oh no way."

Turning in the direction of my building I get the creepy feeling again. Rubbing my neck as I look around, but people were going about their business as usual, no one was just watching me.

Entering my building through the back entrance, I stop at the mailboxes to check my mail. Just the usual utility bill and an advertisement for a new coffee shop. Glancing out the front door as I turn to the stairs I notice a man entering the vacant building across the street. Maybe they were going to start working on it.

After my usual walk through I shrug out of my jacket and head for the closet. Look like a geek.

Seriously. What was wrong with the way I normally dress? Flipping through my meager collection of clothes. "Oh what's the use. If they take me for anything other than a fellow gamer that's their problem." I pull out black cargos, a grey tee shirt, my black boots and a hoodie. After my shower and dressing in my 'geek gear' I pull my hair into a ponytail before taking my contacts out and sliding my glasses on. Looking in the mirror, good enough.

Checking the time I really didn't have enough to get into reading or looking through more files so I plop on the couch, turning the TV on. Flipping through the stations to see if there was any news on the killings but all was quiet.

Rubbing my neck I look at the window, it was getting dark out but I still feel like someone was watching. Turning the lamp off I go to the window. Looking out I take in the street below which was filled with people heading home from work. Lights were coming on in other apartments across the street, streetlights were coming on. Turning my eyes to the roof across from me a shudder crawls up my back. What is it about that building that creeps me out? Pulling the drapes closed just as my phone dings, a text from Ron they were leaving the station now, so they'd be here in a minute.

Turning the lamp back on and leaving the TV on low, I start to tuck my weapon in the back of my pants then stop, there was no way I could take it into a club so I slip it back into my nightstand instead grabbing my pepper spray.

Running down the stairs, Ron pulls up just as I open the front door.

><

She shuts the drapes again. She must be in for the night. He lowers the binoculars thinking he can go hunting, try to find another gift since the last one wasn't good enough. He needs to find another conquest from the dark so that the way to the wall will be clear. He needs to finish killing the dark knights. Wait! Is that her coming out the front door? No that one wears glasses, his pretty doesn't need glasses for her beautiful dark eyes and she's getting into a car his pretty doesn't need a car. Her powerful legs carry her everywhere she needs.

143

His pretty, it will be soon, soon that he will have met the requirements for the prize. Soon my pretty soon!

><

Joey looks over the seat at Grace. "Hum. Pretty good I must say. You do look geekish."

With as much sarcasm as I can manage. "Gee thanks. But I don't see that Ron made much effort at all." Since he was dressed in exactly the same thing he had when I left them earlier.

"No time. Besides I look good, I always look good."

"Sheesh." Deciding a change of subject was needed. "So tell me what you found out."

Joey turns to face me. "We checked all of the vics homes. Each one had the game on their TV's the only one that was on computer was the programmer. Each one had reached the top level of the purchased game, and the programmer was the only one that had managed to hack into the back to reach the other levels. They all had avatars with some really wicked names. And I found one lord that was in all the levels they were playing. His name is Hanzor. I must say he's pretty wicked with the sword. He pretty much demolished everyone."

"So he could be the one? Hanzor?"

"Could be." Joey grins. "We have earplugs in to hear each other in the club. We won't be able to stick together totally." He reaches back and drops a com into my hand. I wasn't going to correct his terminology on it. Tucking it into my ear making sure some of my curls covered it.

Ron clears his throat. "Anything from the dentist?"

"Besides an appointment? He says it's a front tooth from a young male. He took a small sample and is going to run DNA. He'll get it to me as soon as he can."

Ron nods as he pulls into the parking lot behind the ZoneRoom. There weren't many cars there. "Doesn't seem to be many people here."

Joey opens the car door. "Most people walk or cab it, not many people drive that live right in town."

I started to ask why he didn't drive but at that moment Ron grabs my hand. "We're going to be a couple tonight."

"A couple of what?"

Ron gives me a look of dumbfoundedness, Joey laughs. "She got you dude, you should see your face."

Giving Ron a huge smile as I bump his arm. "Relax."

We enter the building to what I would consider total confusion. Joey leads us to a high table with two men sitting at it. He bumps fists with them both before leaning close to talk to them, they look at us then nod. Joey hands both of us clip on tags as he attaches his to his collar. Following his example we follow as he leads the way into the dim room.

The whole place was painted black even the floor was black. Tables were set up every few feet with either computers or laptops. Along the walls were huge monitors with tables in front for the players and there had to be at least a hundred people busily playing games. Most had on headphones, but a few had the sound on making a weird noise throughout the room.

Everyone was dressed in either loose jeans or yoga pants, even the men. Baggy tee shirts or hoodies was the norm along with either boots or designer athletic shoes. Hats, beanies and baseball caps covered every head and most wore glasses or sunglasses.

Chapter 18

Joey leads us to the stairway so we could go to the Game of Conquest floor. Again everything was painted black but the lighting here was nonexistent, the ambient light from the computer screens was the only illumination in the room. Everyone had on earphones so the only noise was moans and groans from the players, occasionally a happy yell and the click of computer keys.

I take a place behind a couple that were so engrossed in the game an explosion wouldn't have phased them. Soon I was engulfed in what they were doing on the screen, they had the knights running for their life, the lords were being killed at record speed. When the young man raises both arms in victory I move on to other players, standing behind a man with a hoodie that completely covered his face. But the odor from him made me move on quickly. Putting my finger under my nose as I walk away, wow ever heard of soap?

Meeting up with Ron who was standing behind Joey watching as he crucifies the lords he had trapped on the screen. "I thought he wasn't allowed to play anymore."

"He was able to take the spot of a young lady that got sick." I follow his eyes to a small woman near the bar that was sipping water. Her face did look a little green even in this lighting.

Nodding at him I turn my attention back to Joey, he had Hanzor trapped. Watching as he backs Hanzor against the side of a building they engage in a vicious sword fight with Hanzor doing some wicked moves but he didn't have the moves that Joey had and with one last swing of his sword, he kills Hanzor. As the avatar falls to the ground the man with body odor stands and screams, throwing his controller to the floor before he turns and runs down the stairs.

Looking over at Ron he nods and we start to follow only to be blocked by the players that were now standing watching as the man flees.

"Excuse us! Move! Out of the way!" Ron pushes people as we try to get to the staircase. Once we were down the stairs we were blocked again by people watching. Of course we lost him.

Joey meets us at the door where we were looking up and down the street. But it was so dark there was no way we would see anyone. "Man that was wicked." The smile on his face told the reason people got so engrossed on these games, Joey was on a high that had nothing to do with drugs.

Ron turns in a circle with his hands on his hips. "Did anyone get a look at this face?"

Taking the com out of my ear. "No but I got a good whiff of his cologne." Getting two puzzled looks. "The man hasn't been acquainted with a shower in months."

><

He lost! He was killed. Someone is coming for him! He needs to get the gifts for his pretty faster. He wasn't going to be beat! Running as hard as he can to the one place he feels safe. He needs to get more gifts! He needs to please his pretty before the knights come for him.

He runs onto a busy street slowing down as he encounters more people, slowing down more as he scans the crowd. He needs someone with dark hair and eyes, he needs someone quick! There! A dark haired man coming from the coffee shop. He gets behind the man, he gets close, he waits until they approach an alley then he pushes the man into it. He pushes the man in front of him, pushing his hood off he pulls the knife from the sheath on his back. His present was on the ground holding his hands in front of his face, he's asking for help, he has no chance. He holds the knife over his head, seeing the lord that killed him in front of him he takes the knife and swings down, making contact with the present, again and again he makes contact until there was nothing left. Wiping the knife on the present he smiles, she will be happy with this gift. Feeling relief of undoing what happened at the game he briskly walks toward home to plan the next present. He wasn't finished yet.

><

Walking back to the car Joey asks. "So what's next?"

"For you bro, home. For Grace, home. For me, home. Tomorrow we'll tackle it again."

We're all quiet as Ron takes the expressway to his parent's house to drop Joey off when the radio squawks. After the radio quiets from informing us of a gruesome murder on Bright Street which is about five blocks from the ZoneRoom, Ron hits the lights while making a very illegal u-turn on the expressway heading back to town and the scene.

When we reach the street to find it was blocked, Ron pulls as close to the curb as he can, leaving the lights on as we get out. Ron tells Joey to stay with the car.

"Are you kidding? No way."

"Then you don't touch anything, don't say anything and don't give your opinion." Ron was giving him his 'don't mess with the cop' attitude. Joey nods his understanding before following us down the street.

Several clusters of officers were interviewing witnesses along with a handful of detectives. The entrance to the alley was roped off with an ambulance waiting. I see Dr. Mellon making his way through the crowd of people, waving his hand in the air at questions being thrown at him.

The captain was trying to create a little calm but wasn't having much luck. Approaching him from behind, Ron clears his throat. "Captain."

The captain turns to face us a little relief washes over his face. "Thank goodness. I need you two to look at the victim and see if we should consider this one part of the serial killers work." He nods in the direction of the alley.

With a nod we duck under the tape walking along the side of the alley. Forensics was working down the center and around the body. Approaching slowly since I wasn't a fan if dead bodies but Ron charges ahead joining the detective that was standing over the body with a handkerchief over his nose and mouth.

Feeling Joey leaning on me a little to see the body over my shoulder I move closer. It appears to be a young man with dark hair but that was about all I could tell, the amount of blood covering him told me he had a violent end. Edging a little closer I feel Joey's breath on my neck. "Joey please give me some room."

"Oh sorry." He backs up a step or two but was still leaning close.

Pulling as much air as I can in my lungs, I clamp my mouth shut then take the three steps to the body. Oh My Lord. Closing my eyes I say a quick prayer before opening them again to the horror before me.

The young man was lying on his back, his arms and legs spread out. His arms were nothing but mangled skin and muscle, his torso was cut to shreds with one long slash across his throat. I say another prayer then turn away thankful that I hadn't eaten anything.

Joining the captain along with the detective at the alley entrance. "Captain do we know anything yet on his identity?"

Looking at his notebook. "Sean Parker, age nineteen, had stopped at Brewster's for a coffee after his last class." He nods to a little cluster of kids. "His friends were about a hundred yards ahead, they saw him come out of the shop then started walking up the street waiting for him to catch up. When he didn't catch up to them, they backtracked and found him in the alley." He shakes his head. "Horrible." Looking at me, "Any ideas?"

Letting a breath out. "Only one." I look around at all the people within earshot. "I can give you a detailed report tomorrow." Giving me a nod of understanding as he watches the EMT's carrying the black body bag out of the alley with most of the forensics team following.

Joey comes to stand beside me, his face a lot more somber than before and he was extremely quiet. "See you at the car."

It never gets easy to see murder, but that had to have been his first experience. Looking back to see Ron making his way to me. "Gruesome. Let's go."

Walking a little slower than when we arrived, I follow him back to the car. Once we were all inside Ron says. "If that's our guy, he's losing it."

"I know we aren't sure yet, but if Hanzor was the guy at the club and he's the killer, he'll feel like he's not in control anymore, he'll start getting sloppy like tonight if he killed that boy. He'll be more reckless, not as discriminating on his prey or gifts. But he's also going to take anyone that strikes his fancy or he feels is a threat now. He'll escalate."

Ron smacks the steering wheel. "So what we just wait and let him kill again and again?"

Joey clears his throat. "So me killing him in the game resulted in that kids' death?"

Ron claps his hand on his brother's shoulder. "No. Don't ever think that. This guy is a psychopath, there's no telling what he'll do or what will set him off."

"But he ran after I killed him. Then that kid was dead."

I lean forward. "Joey the only thing that you did was point him out to us. That's a good thing. Now all we have to do is find him." Turning to Ron. "Think we need to get this out to the media now. They need to be aware."

He lets out his breath. "We'll let the captain make that call." Tapping the steering wheel more. "I wish there was a way we could trace him."

Joey sits up straight. "Wait. I can get in the game and find Hanzor again, if I find him I can trace where he's originating from." He slaps his thighs. "The club! They have cameras all over that place and I mean all over."

"We need a warrant for that."

"Take me home. I can access from there. They contracted me a few months again when they thought they had a hacker, I still have permission to go into their databanks."

Ron cranks the engine with a smile. "That's my little bro." Whipping the car around. "Still want to go home Grace?"

"No I want to see that footage too."

Breaking every speed limit between downtown and the subdivision that Joey lived in, we were there in fifteen minutes. Instead of going to the front door, Joey hightails it around the house to a basement door. Easing the door open he puts his finger to his lips. "Quiet until we're in my lair."

I start to laugh. His lair. So cute. Once we were in his office, he shuts the door. "This room is soundproofed so I won't bother mom." Sitting down in front of the largest of the monitors he clicks a few keys. Seconds later the inside of the club appears. Joey fast forwards until the time was just a couple of hours before we had arrived. Slowing the tape down of the front door, we watch, looking for the hoodie. But with so many of the gamers wearing hoodies that wasn't going to work.

"Is there a view of the table he was sitting at?"

Joey closes his eyes for a minute. "Okay the camera over the staircase should have him then." We watch as he forwards until you could see us then he follows me as I watch the two gamers then move on to the stinky guy.

Pointing to the screen. "That's him."

Joey changes the angle just a little then zooms in. You couldn't make out his face but we had a good profile picture. Also you could see old scrapes on his knuckles. We watch as he plays Joey then his avatar is killed, he stands up and we had a good shot of his face. "Bingo!" Capturing the guys face he sends it to another monitor, slowly he diminishes the darkness, clears up the blurs and we had a picture. A clear picture. We know what our guy looks like.

Dark hair falls onto his forehead, his eyes are slanted just a little but are dark, very dark, a scar through his left eyebrow. A nicely shaped nose with cheeks a little sunken and a nicely shaped chin with another scar on the left side. And he looks familiar. "Can I have a copy of that?"

Joey prints me a copy and one for Ron too, which he flips in front of my face. "You know we can't legally use this."

"Yes we can. Joey is technically an employee of the club. He has a business license, I'm assuming." I get a nod from Joey. "We're using this as a person of interest in a felony. Perfectly legal." I poke him in the chest. "Remember Criminal of Justice degree." Ron actually gets a little childish and sticks his tongue out at me. "Can we go now. I'm wiped out."

"Sure." Taking Joey's hand. "Thanks man, you were a huge help tonight."

"It was awesome. Well except for the body."

Ron holds his hand out, Joey looks a little confused before he sighs. "Man you are no fun." Taking his ear com out and placing it in Ron's hand.

Letting ourselves out, we're quiet as we get back in the car. Heading back toward Boston I feel like the demon isn't as strong as he was before. We were on the right track and he was losing power.

Ron lets me off at the back street of my building. "Thanks. Tomorrow morning?"

"Yeah. And tonight I'm devouring a chocolate cake I bought the other day."

With a smile I leave the vehicle shutting the door quietly. Unlocking the back door and taking the stairs, when I reach my landing I stand for a second. All was quiet as it should be at 4am. Entering my apartment, I do my usual look under the bed before locking the door.

Putting the picture on the coffee table, I take one more look before heading for the shower.

Stopping in my tracks I turn back to the picture.

Now I know who is reminds me of.

Chapter 19

The morning couldn't get here fast enough and I couldn't wait. Kicking the covers free I throw on clothes, grab my bag and the photo, fill a to-go mug of coffee and leave the building. Okay so it was barely 6am but I needed to dig a little more with this new information that has arisen.

The station was quiet when I entered, the night crew was still here finishing their shift. I wave at a couple of the officers as I pass on my way to my office. Unlocking the door I happen to see a light coming from underneath the door to the old conference room. Dumping my things on my desk I head for the conference room when I open the door to find Ron standing in front of the whiteboard. He had attached the ME's photo of the victim from last night and also the photo of the man from the club.

"You couldn't sleep either huh?" I ask as I stand beside him.

"No. Something was really bothering me so I came back in." He flicks at the photo that Joey had given us. "Why does he looks familiar?"

"I know. Wait." Leaving the conference room I head for the front room where there was a picture of every detective that worked for the precinct. Grabbing a frame from the wall I carry it back to the conference room and prop it beside the photo.

Ron looks at the framed photo and then the other. "No way." His voice was a whisper. "It can't be." Turning to me. "Can it?"

Shrugging my shoulders. "Could be. But we need to be careful on how we confirm it. If they have any kind of communication with each other I don't want them to know we're checking into them." Picking the framed photo up I take it back to the wall and re-hang it, making sure no one was watching me. Back in the conference room I find Ron was now sitting down shaking his head. Sitting across from him. "Are you okay?"

"No." Leaning forward his eyes penetrate mine. "How could this be? If they look that much alike it has to be a brother."

"Yes. We need to check his file to see if one is listed first. Maybe he had other family we can ask without bringing suspicion to him."

Now having a purpose Ron slides his chair back and gets up. "I can find that out."

As he leaves the conference room my eyes slide to the whiteboard and the photo of Sean. So young, so much life yet to live and all for being in the wrong place at the wrong time. With a sigh I head back to my office making sure the conference room door locked behind me.

Once I had replenished my coffee mug I settle behind my desk and start writing down what we knew about the killer, which wasn't much. But it was more than we had. My phone rings, looking at it to see Dr. Shaw's name. Answering the call. "Dr. Shaw, it isn't Tuesday yet is it?"

With a laugh, "No you're safe. But I thought you'd like to know that I got the DNA. Do you want to come back and get the report?"

"I do. I'll be there shortly and thanks so much." Grabbing my jacket I write a hasty note for Ron before shutting my office door.

Leaving the station by the front door, I high-tail it to the office building where Dr. Shaw's office was. Once I had the report I could have Dr. Mellon run a comparison and hope that our killer was in the database. Pushing the door open to the dentist's office to find Dr. Shaw standing at the counter talking to Michelle and Joyce. "Good morning."

Dr. Shaw turns to me with a smile. "Grace, that was fast." He hands me an envelope which I clutch.

"Thank you so much."

Turning to leave, Michelle adds. "See you Tuesday."

I groan loudly as I leave the office, with all of them laughing. Clutching the envelope I make it back to the station in record time. Entering the morgue I find Dr. Mellon talking to his secretary. Looking up at I enter. "Grace. Good morning, what brings you by so early?"

Holding the envelope up. "A favor please."

With a nod I follow him into his office. "Now how can I help you?"

Handing him the envelope. "I have DNA that I would like ran through the system and without anyone knowing."

"Legal?"

"Doc."

He smiles then motions for me to follow him. We enter the inner chamber of where he does his magic. Sliding the report from the envelope he places it into a scanner of sorts before turning a computer on, a few seconds later the DNA comes up on the screen, he clicks a few times with a mouse and the program starts. "This may take some time you know. Why don't I call you if I get a result?"

Not wanting to leave but knowing what he said was right, I put my hand on the doorknob. "Thanks, I'd appreciate it." But before I had a chance to turn the knob the computer dings.

"My that was fast." The doctor looks at the screen. "Sorry Grace, no match in the system."

"Thanks for trying doc."

Well that was a bust but maybe Ron had better luck, hopefully. Back in my office I plop down in my chair contemplating the next actions we needed to take. We still haven't been to the old movie theater where the piece of the poster could have come from.

Ron enters my office with two cups of coffee. Sitting down he props his feet on the edge of my desk before taking a sip.

"Well?"

"Nothing in his files on family. Dead end."

"Drat so was the tooth DNA. So let's visit that old movie theater you were talking about."

Lowering his feet. "Yeah I forgot about that. Ready?"

"Yes."

Both of us slide our jackets on as I shut and lock my office. Leaving by the side entrance I follow Ron's lead by turning left. Walking down Bright Street then Logan and then Conway we wind up one street over from my building. Stopping in front of a three storied concrete building that had definitely seen better days. Most of the front windows were now covered in plywood, the ticket office was crumbling with all the glass broken.

Ron pushes on one of the three doors that led inside and surprise, surprise it opens. We enter the building directly into the lobby where the concession stand had been. Sweeping my flashlight around the room my first thought is a perfect place for a horror movie. But I did notice footprints in the dust on the floor, lots of footprints.

"Ron look at the floor."

Shining his flashlight around then he squats, studying the prints. "Hum they look like they're from the same boot. We need to be careful where we step."

The doors into the theater itself were long gone so we walk directly into a huge cavernous room with no seats. I assume they had been taken out when the theater closed. We each walk the slanted floor to the middle of the room.

Ron takes a few sniffs. "What's that smell? It's gross."

I take a whiff and immediately regret it. "Something's rotten in here, maybe a dead rat or two."

"Well I hope we don't run across it."

We each take a different side of the room looking for anything. But the most interesting thing we found was an old pair of binoculars. Making our way to the stage we immediately stop and back away. The middle of the wooden stage was where some of the odor was coming from because the center of the stage was the color of dried blood, and a massive amount of dried blood.

Pulling his cell out he calls it in asking for CSU and forensics before he calls the captain.

Walking around the edge of the stage I shine my light up into the three storied ceiling to see ropes dangling that were dark in color in places. Oh Lord, have we found where he's killing them?

The movie screen was long gone, but tattered curtains still hung dividing the stage in half. Walking behind the curtain to find barrel upon barrel lined up against the back wall. The odor was much stronger back here. Approaching the first metal barrel I find the top was strapped in place with a slide lock. Pushing the lock open, I lift the lid letting it drop to the floor, the odor is overwhelming and I knew even before looking in what was in the barrel. To make sure I shine my light in and then turn around, thankful I hadn't eaten.

Chapter 20

Ron comes running around the curtain. "Grace what is it?"

I was still bending over waiting for the wave of nausea to pass so I just motion behind me to the barrel.

"Oh Good Lord." He starts coughing then joins me. Pulling my arm. "Let's get out of here."

I let him pull me to the front of the stage where I sit on the edge taking deep breaths. "I believe we have found his killing place."

Ron sits down beside me. "I think you're right. But there must be twenty barrels back there. Do you think they all have bodies in them?"

Nodding before answering him. "Yes. He probably practiced before he had the way he wanted to kill them down to his satisfaction." Taking more deep breaths. "If you noticed the throat was cut deep enough to sever the head, the throat slashes on the victims we found weren't that deep."

"Sorry I didn't look that close."

We both raise our heads as we hear voices coming from the lobby. Getting up we meet the techs and the captain before they come into the room. First to explain the footprints and then our find on the stage and behind the curtain.

The captain's face tightens as he directs the techs to start then to shut the front of the building so those curious folks that when they see the yellow tape immediately stick their heads in.

Rejoining us at the edge of the lobby he asks. "Tell me why you looked here and exactly what you've found."

A bottle of water magically appears before mine and Ron's faces, with a nod thanking the tech that had handed them to us. I take a long sip before turning my attention back to the captain. "We found a scrap of an old movie poster at the equipment shed on the pier. As clean as the shed was that shouldn't have been there and it was under the machine that the victim had been chained to, so we took a hunch and came here." Taking another sip of water. "When we got here we pushed what was left of the door open and this is what we found. This is probably his killing site and once he sees that we've violated it he's going to escalate."

"So killing that young man in the alley was escalation?"

"That was pure anger. It was sloppy, messy and uncharacteristic of his rituals." A thought occurs to me. "May I make a suggestion?"

The captain nods at me. "Go ahead."

"We get as much evidence as we can to run tests on, some of the blood from the stage and whatever they can get from the barrels, fingerprints, anything then set up cameras in here and leave with 24 hour surveillance on the building and the cameras."

"Good idea. But what if he doesn't come back here since we've been inside he's bound to know."

Shaking my head. "I don't think so. He acts under the cover of night. I noticed that in the games, everything happened at night."

I watch as the captain mulls this over for a few minutes before looking at this watch. "Well we can't hide our footprints on the floor but maybe he won't notice in the dark."

"We'll just have to take that chance."

Finally he nods. "Okay we'll try. I'll call to get the IT guys to set up cameras and move the techs along a little, it'll be dark in two hours so we need to be out of here by then."

><

He watches as they enter his sanctuary, his killing field. He screams. Where will he take his presents now? Where can he do the ritual now? He screams. Everything was fine until his pretty was with the other man, the other lord, the opposition that's trying to win her to the other side. He screams. He needs to fix this. He needs to conquer the opposition, he needs to act now. He screams.

><

Ron and I move outside to the front of the building to wait on the IT techs and to get some fresh air. Leaning on the building I ask Ron. "Are you in agreement with me?"

Propping one foot on the side of the building. "I do, but I don't think he'll be back here."

"Why not?"

Shrugging. "If he's so perceptive that he dumps the bodies at night with no witnesses, no trace of evidence, no nothing, he's going to know as soon as he goes through the door that someone has been here."

Good point there, which makes me think that we need to do this a different way. "Random entrance from a stranger he's going to see it as the opposition but what if we put a huge sold sign across the front of the building. He'll still go in to check where he performed his killings to see if they're still there. He may even take the barrels out but he won't be angry, he'll see that as a challenge to find another place."

The IT guys pull up in their boring white van, Greg gets out with a huge smile. "Grace, Detective, We hear that you need a little camera magic here."

"Hi Greg, yes we do, Ron will fill you in." I take off across the street where there was a realtor's office hoping that they may have a sold banner lying around. Opening the door I'm immediately met with several "Hello, how can we help you'. Picking the closest agent I pull my badge out. "I was wondering if we could borrow a Sold Banner."

The man that I had chosen to talk to smiles as he gets up. "Sure we do, it has the company logo on it, will that be a problem?"

"Not unless it bothers you." Plastering my biggest smile on. "We'll only need it a few days, we're doing some work and really want to keep people out." I nod across the street.

Following my nod. "We were wondering what was going on. Anything we should be worried about?"

Thinking quickly. "No. It seems as if the previous owner left some props and things that are questionable and we're just making sure that it's disposed of correctly. Nothing to be worried about."

His smile diminishes a little at my statement but hopefully enough that it won't raise concerns. Handing me a large plastic roll. "Whenever you're finished with it, just being it on back."

Thanking him I leave the office re-crossing the street to find that the tech guys were done and had parked the van on a side street. Ron was watching me with a frown. "Where did you go? They're done placing a few cameras and are setting up in the van now."

Handing him the roll. "Let's get this up across the front, hopefully that will explain the presence of other people being here today."

After we get the Sold sign draped across the front of the building and the captain and tech team came out, we head for the white van as the rest of the crew leaves.

Climbing into the van we find Greg in his element with all four screens showing the inside of the theater the lobby, the inside, the stage and the back. We had a good view of anyone that comes in. I crawl into a chair tucking my legs under me while Ron hovers then starts pacing the tiny space.

"Ron either sit or go." Evidently it had already gotten on Greg's nerves.

Stopping his three step pace before putting his hands on his hips. "I can't just sit here and wait. Is anyone hungry I can go get some food."

We both give him several suggestions before he leaves the cramped space.

Greg snorts. "Guy is claustrophobic."

Chapter 21

Greg and I settle into a comfortable silence with him checking his phone every few minutes while I was thinking through everything again. Finding the bodies in the barrels was a definite twist to things. Why weren't the people reported missing? With that many people gone it should have raised flags unless they were homeless, which would explain why the police wouldn't be looking for twenty missing people.

Night had fallen, the streetlights were on and the people population has dwindled down to just a few here and there. We know our guy likes to do things late at night so we probably have a long night ahead of us.

Ron sure was taking his time bringing food back to us and Greg must have been thinking the same thing because he says. "Wonder where Ron went to get us food?"

A light knock on the side door before it opens with Ron climbing in carrying several large bags. The odor of food fills the van making my stomach growl in earnest. Setting all the bags on one of the two empty seats left, Ron sits down sipping from a large cup. "What are you drinking?"

Giving me a glare before answering. "Tea."

I knew then that he was drinking chamomile tea which calms him down so I leave that alone. "What's for dinner?"

"Little bit of everything you asked for. Burgers, wraps from Spencer's, chili from Z's and hot dogs from Teo's food truck and he gave us a deal since he was shutting down for the night."

Greg makes a dive for the bag of hot dogs while I dug until I found some wraps. Thanking Ron for going to all the trouble, we settle back with our food, eyes glued to the monitor which was getting really boring now that most people were off the streets now and this being a business area there were few apartments.

Once we had eaten with Greg doing the most damage, Ron takes the trash out to the alley we

were parked beside and dumps it. While he was gone
we see a slim hooded figure with his hands shoved
in his pants pockets approach the theater with his
head down, when he gets to the door he stops, I
suppose reading the sign. Taking a step back he
looks up before tucking his head again and walking
off. His clothes look ragged and worn to me so I
was marking him off as homeless.

For the next four hours we alternated between
watching the monitor and Greg playing, with nothing
else happening unless we needed to bring in the cat
that curled up in the corner beside the door for
the night.

><

*He takes a chance going to the building but he
wanted to see what they had done inside but when he
gets to the door he sees something that tells him
not to bother. A Sold sign was stretched across the
doors, his altar was gone! Leaving he keeps his
scream in, he knows someone is watching, he feels
it, it must be one of the lords. He needs to stay
hidden tonight.*

><

Glancing at the time on the monitor for the thousandth time, I stretch and yawn. "Sorry guys, let's call it a night. If he hasn't come by now he isn't going to show tonight."

Greg pushes his glasses to his forehead before rubbing his eyes. "Good idea, getting a killer headache." Sliding his glasses back down he crawls to the driver's seat. Ron slides over next to me as the van pulls away from the curb.

"Think that was our guy?"

"I've been thinking on that. If it was he's calmer than I would think, I mean we soiled his altar by being in there that should have made him angry. So I'm inclined to believe it was someone looking for a place to sleep tonight."

Greg pulls up at the back entrance to my building. "See you in the morning." I say automatically.

"No you'll see me later today. I definitely need to get some sleep before we tackle anything else."

Looking at my watch, 3:45am. "You're right. See you later then." Pulling the side door open, my legs complain from sitting so long as I get out. Sliding the door closed I wave before turning to unlock the back door. Entering the building to eerie silence, no TV's blaring, no kids playing, no one leaving or entering. Unlocking my apartment door, I go through my routine before shutting the door, making sure it was dead bolted before kicking my shoes off.

I had left my bag at the office so that left watching TV or actually reading a book instead of files. After a quick shower I crawl under the covers, laying there thinking of what we had found today. It was times like this that I wish I had a pet, a cat to cuddle with or a dog that liked to burrow under the covers with me but with my work schedule it wouldn't be fair to leave a pet locked inside an apartment all day.

Picking up a book from my nightstand, it was on abnormalities in the mind of a psychotic adult, no way, too serious and too deep. Digging down further in the pile I find a paperback that Sheila had given me months ago saying it would make me forget the horrors of my day. I start reading and it did make me forget my day and turn my thoughts to witches and warlocks, it almost made me so sleepy that I couldn't hold the book any longer.

Waking to bright sunshine, I look at the clock on my nightstand, it was 11:45am. I haven't slept this late in years. Stretching I think that even the demon had left me alone last night.

Getting up the first thing I do is start a pot of coffee before throwing open the drapes to let in the sunshine. It was going to be a glorious day and I thank the Lord for that.

After getting dressed I decide to spend some time with my Bible, reading in Romans 8 about glory, justification and salvation and it was uplifting.

After my second mug of coffee I fix a to-go cup and leave with every intention of going straight to work but once I was outside I decide to detour and go past the movie theater just to see if anything had changed after we left.

It was only a six or seven block walk to the area so it didn't take long to get there. Standing across the street there wasn't anything different so I turn and head back toward work.

Chapter 22

As I enter the station Ron runs right into me,
holding his arms out to catch me before I fell.
"Grace I'm sorry. Another body was found come on."

Turning to follow him. "Where?"

"The old sewing factory. Female, early
forties, ripped open like Sean."

Slowing down as we reach the car, I slide in
the passenger seat. As Ron speeds through lights
making short time to the scene, I was thinking that
this probably wasn't connected to our guy. Unless
he was getting desperate.

When Ron turns onto 8th street, we find it
practically blocked so he pulls over at the first
place he can. Getting out I take in the other
buildings close by, a coffee shop, bakery, dry
cleaners, a couple of stores. The rest were
brownstones and converted factories. Just like the
rest.

Ducking under the police tape we enter the
brightly lit entrance to the building where the

victim was lying under a yellow tarp. Looking around I think this can't be right.

The forensics tech nods to Ron and me before lifting the tarp off the body. Straight short light blonde hair, blue eyes, she had slight wrinkles around her eyes, so she smiled a lot. Her bag, a briefcase, a carry all bag, a cup of coffee and her phone were lying close. Zip ties had secured her hands and ankles, a gag stuffed in her mouth. Dozens of knife slashes crisscrossed her body with one deep cut through the throat. She never knew what happened or had a chance.

As the detectives and techs went over the scene, the only thing I could think of was that he was going off. He was losing it, getting desperate. Maybe his pretty had rejected him, maybe he saw her with someone else. But he was escalating.

Ron comes to stand beside me. "Gruesome. Remind me again why I like being a detective."

"To catch people that do this. But it feels off." Gesturing to the door. "It's like he pulled her straight off the street with no plan. She wasn't stalked, she wasn't chosen. And the killing is messy. He would have left blood soaked yet no one saw anything. No reports. No calls of suspicious activity."

One of the ME's guys came over. "Hey Grace. Looks like she may be been dead for three to four days. We also found drag marks from the door, so it appears she was dragged in." Ron cocks an eyebrow at me. "I'll let Dr. Mellon fill you in on anything else he finds." Tipping his head at us, he walks away.

Mulling over what he had told us I knew that this was him, something had made him angry, something he didn't like. Maybe his pretty is rejecting him, maybe she made fun of him. We needed to up our game now.

Leaving the techs to finish processing the scene we return to the station to find the mayor and the captain having words in the captain's office. Ron looks at me. "Think we need to interrupt?"

"Definitely."

The captain sees us approaching his office and opens the door. "Grace, Detective. Please tell us you have something."

The mayor sits down on the couch while Ron and I each take a chair with the captain standing behind his desk.

Ron gives me a pleading look so clearing my throat I start. "Mayor." He nods at me but his expression clearly said this better be good. "We think that the same man is committing all of these murders, we also think we know what he looks like but don't have an identity, yet. We also believe that he is going through his own ritual and invading the theater where he performed it has escalated him." I see the captain sit down from the corner of my eye. "There's a game called Game of Conquest that each of the six victims played, we also believe they were involved in a club called ZoneRoom and this is where our suspect found his victims. The prize in the game is a woman, a dark haired, dark eyed woman, the more lords that are killed wins the damsel. I think he's playing the game in real life. There are other similarities that I would prefer not to mention right now and mayor I don't believe it would be a good idea to hold a press conference and divulge this information yet. I think that will make him kill more randomly and the outcome would cause panic and possibly a few vigilantes to surface."

Holding my breath as the mayor stares at me. He was known to cause controversy and has made numerous blunders through the six years he's been mayor. So I was nervous on what his reaction was going to be. "I agree. We need to keep as much information as possible quiet, but I will need to give some kind of statement. These last two killings were brutal and we need to answer to the public as soon as possible to quell any fears they may have." This was a different approach for him. "Grace I'm asking that you please write up a statement and be prepared to deliver it tomorrow." The mayor stands giving the captain a slight smile. "I apologize for what I said earlier, you were right I don't want to cause a panic." Nodding at all of us in turn the mayor leaves, all of us letting out the breath we had been holding.

"Whew." The captain wipes his brow with a cloth. "Grace I'm depending on you to deliver a concise statement without divulging too much information."

"Yes sir. I'll get it ready now."

"Oh and Grace?"

"Yes sir."

"The woman they found today was the mayor's niece, so he'll play by our rules for now."

With nothing left to say, Ron and I leave the office making tracks for mine. Once we were inside, Ron melts. "That was close."

"You think? Now I have to write a statement that doesn't give anything away." Sitting behind my desk I grab a pen then pull my legal pad closer. My phone pings just as I start to write, "It's from Dr. Mellon, he wants to see us."

We head for the basement hoping that there was some good news coming our way. Pushing the door open to the morgue we find the doc waiting for us. "Almost record time but not quite." He motions for us to follow him.

In the morgue he leads us to a table covered with a white cloth, I knew he didn't have time to autopsy the young woman so this must be Sean. "After going over this young man, I noticed something and to be honest if the killer hadn't been so sloppy this time I would have missed it like I did with the others." He removes the cloth the he points to the neck as he turns the overhead light on. "See this little groove? It's a mark on the blade of the knife he's using and it's more of a machete than a knife. Roughly fifteen inches long with a blade that gets larger at the hilt. But this mark I believe is an engraving on the blade." Motioning for us to follow him, he leads us to a computer, opening a file, a large picture comes up. Selecting a portion of the photo he enlarges it. "See here." He points to a mark at the edge of the wound before enlarging it more. An emblem of sorts appears and I remember seeing that in the game. "That's the mark of a knight."

"What?" Both Ron and doc say.

"In the game. The swords of the knights had designs on them, like that." I point to the photo.

"He's engraved his weapon of choice to bear the mark of the knight."

Doc rubs his face. "Okay. Anyway I went back with a magnifying glass on the others that are still here and found what could be the same mark on them. It took a little bit of searching since he was more careful with those killings than this one." He nods at the empty table. "When I have the young lady I'll check to see if the wounds are the same."

"Thanks doc, that helps quite a bit." Leaving the ME to continue his work we leave the morgue, both of us quiet until we reach my office.

Ron starts pacing a little before I ask. "What are you thinking?"

"Wondering if there's a way to pull him out. Maybe announcing a Game of Conquest competition or needing players to test a new version."

I shake my head before he gets too caught up in his musings. "Sorry I don't think that will work. He isn't playing the game, he's living the game. The only thing he wants is the prize, the damsel, the pretty. So offering a competition or a game upgrade won't intrigue him." I think for a minute. "But the idea of meeting the damsel may. If we can announce that the woman will be maybe at ZoneRoom for a special appearance may bring him out."

Rubbing his hands together, Ron sits down in a chair in front of my desk. "So how do we do that without bringing the whole town into the club?"

"The only people that would be interested would be the actual players of the game and we'd need to talk to the owners of ZoneRoom first to see if they'd be willing to do this and then we'd need a woman to play the damsel, preferably an undercover cop with dark hair and eyes."

A smile widens on his face. "I do believe I need to go talk to my brother again and run this past him."

"Do that and I'll write up a quick press statement."

With a wave and a purpose, Ron leaves as I start putting to paper what little bit that will be sharable with the public.

Chapter 23

    Rubbing my eyes, finally finishing the press statement the only thing I can think of is coffee. Getting up I stretch my back before grabbing my mug then think of the vile coffee that would be in the break room. Nope, no way. Clearing my desk then grabbing my coat, I head for the side door and the coffee shop across the street.

    Once I had a sip of high voltage caffeine, my head starts clearing. I didn't think the idea of trying to lure him out was going to work but him thinking that the pretty was looking for him might. But how to do that without making some kind of press announcement and that would bring every crazy in the city out.

    An idea starts blooming. Pulling my phone from my pocket I text Ron to forget the idea of ZoneRoom that it wouldn't work then add I may have an idea but we'd talk tomorrow.

Walking slowly toward home I can't help notice the vacant buildings. As I pass one I'd try the door, by the time I reached my block every door I had tried was open for anyone to go into. Maybe I needed to add that to the statement I was going to give to the mayor. These vacant buildings needed to be locked or secured in some way that just anyone couldn't walk in and make it their killing ground or shrine.

Entering my building through the front door, I stop for my mail before heading upstairs. At my apartment I go through my ritual before shutting and locking the door. Taking my last sip of coffee, I toss the cup before heading to my bedroom and a shower. Once I was in some comfortable clothes and sitting in front of the TV, I text Wade to see if he available for breakfast or lunch the next day. I was missing him a little. Laying my phone on the coffee table hoping for a reply soon, I reach back to pull the blanket off the back of the couch when I notice a light from across the street. Getting up I look out the window to the building next door. It was totally dark. Starting to pull the drapes shut,

I notice a slight movement of light on the top floor. Was there someone over there? I stand for several minutes but I don't see the light again, it must have been a reflection. Pulling the drapes, I lay back down on the couch turning my attention to the TV before closing my eyes, thankful the demons were resting tonight.

Waking several hours later feeling refreshed and clear headed I start a pot of coffee before getting dressed. Picking my phone up from the coffee table checking to see if Wade had answered while I was asleep, but no, nothing. Drinking my coffee as I watch the morning news, glad that the night had been quiet, I make a mental note to make a few changes to the statement for the mayor.

Fixing my to-go cup of coffee I head for the office finding Ron waiting impatiently for me outside my office door. "Eager to get going today?"

"A little. Joey and I hashed over some ideas last night on how to get him out. One idea that Joey had…"

I hold my hand up. "What about something simple like on the vacant buildings we know he gravitates to we put up a poster announcing her appearance. That way the entire city won't be involved nor any innocent gamers."

Ron shuts his mouth as he thinks about what I had just proposed. "Huh. Simple yet to the point. That would probably work better than some of the ideas we had last night."

"Okay let me finish this press statement and we'll go see if we can get one made." As I take my coat off I pull my phone out, checking to make sure Wade hadn't texted. Still nothing. That wasn't like him.

Finishing the statement I drop it off at the captain's office before we leave the station.

><

He'd been watching the rock building for hours, a lot of people went in and out and he needed to figure a way to catch the evil one alone. He'd seen him shaking people's hands, even hugging them, he was spreading his evil everywhere. He needed to be stopped. He needed to learn his place. He takes a chance and goes to the back of the rock

198

building. Its old back here, rocks are crumbling, the door to the basement looks like he can push it open, he tries and it opens. He goes in the dark and dank room. There's nothing down here but a few pieces of cast off furniture and it's warm. He leaves the basement to see the evil one coming out the back door with a large black bag. When the evil one sees him he runs at him knocking him to the ground. He drags the evil one to the basement pulling him inside, he shuts the door, he finds something to block the door so no one else can come in. He turns to his prey, the evil one was out cold. That will give him time to secure him. He drags him further into the basement well away from ears and eyes. He knows the rocks will keep any noise from escaping to the outside. He props the evil one against the far wall, he takes the zip ties from his pocket, securing them around the evil ones wrists and ankles. He sits down in front of him, trying to understand why his pretty would want to be with him. But no more, not after he was through.

><

Ron signs a car out so that we could check out the theater and the vacant building from yesterday. There had to be a clue, something that we missed. The captain had assured me that all the barrels were gone so we didn't have to worry about being around a bunch of decomposing bodies and the stench.

We enter to find it the same as we left it, a little disappointing. I take the right side while Ron goes to the left, looking for anything, anything at all.

We knew that the techs had taken samples from the stage and pictures of the footprints, so we weren't being as careful as before.

Lifting up trash to see if there was anything under it, moving empty boxes from behind the concession stand, moving the rotten curtains out of the way. Opening cabinets, even checking out the projection room. Nothing was found but trash even the stage was clear of anything except the bloodstained floor.

I stand in the middle of the stage, I close my eyes imagining being a victim, he has me on the stage, he has me lying on….. wait the sacrifice has to be on an table or altar of some kind. My eyes snap open, so where was it? The blood was in a circle, the very center of the stage was mostly free of blood. There wasn't a table or stand anywhere close. I look up. "Ron!"

I hear him answer from behind the curtains. "Yeah?"

Pointing up. "We need to lower that down."

Coming to stand beside me he looks up. "That? What is it?"

"He was treating the victims as sacrifices, as gifts and to be correct you need an altar." I point up. "That."

Ron goes to the side of the stage where a cluster of ropes were hanging. Untying several trying to find the one that was holding the table up, he finally snags the right one and the table starts to slowly lower. When it settles on the stage it sits directly in the middle of the blood stained floor but the table top was perfectly clear of blood. There was one drawer in the side, taking a glove from his pocket Ron opens the drawer.

Inside was a knife, a bloodied knife not a machete but long and lethal looking. Pulling the knife out, Ron lays it on top of the table. "But this doesn't look like what the doc described."

Taking a hard look at the knife, there were no marks of any kind and it was about half the size of a machete, so no it wasn't what he was using. "No I don't think it is either, but it wouldn't hurt to run it through the lab anyway."

As Ron bags the knife I search further in the drawer, a few zip ties and a couple of dirty rags were the only other things in it. Closing the drawer I take a hard look at the table top. The outline of a body was prominent on the wood along with quite a few knife marks or were they marks from fingernails scratching?

Ron starts taking pictures before calling in what we found, only to get the response that it may be a while, there was a massive traffic accident on the expressway and most available officers were on scene.

I take a picture of the table top myself to add to the collection I was gathering of our suspects profile. When we did catch the guy he was going away for life with what I had so far.

We finish going through the building then decide to get something to eat. Ripping the sold banner down, I take it across the street, thanking the realtors for letting us borrow it. It wasn't going to do any good now since I knew that he wouldn't be back there.

Chapter 24

We stop at a local deli that was famous for its Reuben's. Sitting at a small table in front of the window, we both order Reuben's with chips, Ron adds two cups of coffee.

As we wait for our food, I check my phone again to see if I may have missed a call or text from Wade, but again nothing and that wasn't like him at all. Taking a chance I call his office, his secretary Ann answers on the first ring. "Concord Baptist, how can we help you?" Her voice was a little strained.

"Hi Ann, its Grace. I've been trying to get in touch with Wade and not succeeding. Is he around?"

"Oh Grace, I was just getting ready to call you. We can't find Wade. He was supposed to have a meeting with the Deacons last night and never showed and he's missed the trustees meeting this morning. His Bible study group showed up about fifteen minutes ago and you know how much he enjoys those. I was hoping he was with you or you had heard from him."

My stomach drops to the floor. "I've left several texts for him and tried calling and he hasn't answered. When was the last time you spoke with or saw him?"

"His cell is on his desk and he was here yesterday afternoon when I left at 2pm."

"I'm on my way."

"Thanks Grace."

Filling Ron in on what was going on, he motions for the waitress and cancels our order except for the coffee. Leaving the deli Ron asks. "You don't think Hanzor has him?"

"At this point who knows, but we need to assume that he does."

Driving at a break neck speed we're at the church within ten minutes of leaving the deli. Going to the side entrance where the office is located, I push open the heavy oak door then go down the short hallway to the office. Ann was pacing in front of the windows with the phone to her ear. Catching part of the conversation. "You don't understand, it's not like him to miss anything at church and if he was going to visit someone he would have let me know."

Seeing us enter the office she stops her pacing, approaching her I ask as I nod at the phone. "Police?"

She nods before I take the phone away from here. "This is Grace Hanson. We believe that there may be some foul play concerning the pastor and I know that most officers are at the expressway but we would appreciate maybe one car sent to the Concord Baptist Church." I wait as the dispatcher starts going through her 'it's not a missing person for twenty hour hours spiel. "That's fine, I'll call the captain." Hanging up I immediately dial the captains number, after filling him in on what was going on, he tells me he'll have a patrol car and detective here within the next fifteen minutes.

Handing the phone back to Ann to see that she was losing it fast. Making her sit down while Ron gets her a glass of water, I sit down in the chair in front of her desk. Leaning forward I ask. "Can you tell me everything that went on yesterday?"

She nods before wiping her eyes with a tissue. "Sure. Pastor was in his office when I came in to work as usual, we had coffee as we went over the schedule for yesterday. We looked over the calendar for what was going on this week and he gave me the Bible study outline he wanted me to copy. Uh, he left about 10am to go visit Mrs. Charles in the hospital and he called me when he was leaving to tell me he was stopping by to see Mr. Phelps. When he got here he told me he was going to clean that back storage room out and that's the last I saw him, but I knew he was still here because Ed stopped by to talk to him and I could hear them in the hallway. I left around 2pm but the door to the storage room was open and the back door was open." Tearing the tissue to shreds in her hand, I reach over to pat them.

"We'll find him don't worry but say a prayer." Getting up I motion for Ron to follow me.

Leaving the office I take a left to go down the hall toward the back door. The storage room was at the end of the hall beside the back door, the door was open so I go in.

Looking around at the open boxes and stack of garbage bags I could tell that Wade was tossing most of what was in here. Glancing in a box to see old Sunday school material and a mass of old papers. Attendance records from the 70's, and for some reason it looks like every drawing kids have made since the beginning had been saved.

Leaving the room to stand in front of the back door, I open it looking at the lock before stepping out onto the slate stoop. A large pile of black garbage bags was in a pile at the bottom of the stairs.

Taking the steps slowly with Ron right on my heels, I step onto the grass at the bottom. Nothing strange and no sign of a struggle.

Glancing at the side gate to see it shut with the latch in place. The whole back yard of the church looked normal, no drag marks or even any foot impressions. To the left was the entrance to the basement, remembering Wade saying that work needed to be done at the back of the church and that the basement needed to be closed off entirely

I walk to the door to find the basement locked tight.

Taking in the back of the building understanding what he meant by work needing to be done. A lot of the rock that the church was built from were crumbling, falling down in the grass and in the basement stairwell.

"See anything?" I ask Ron as I take another look around.

"Only that the grass needs cutting and the rock needs to be fixed but nothing that indicates he was taken if that's what you're asking."

"Me either. So where did he go?"

Chapter 25

><

He hears footsteps outside, he waits by the door with a board ready for whoever was thinking of coming inside. Someone tries to open the door, a voice says it's locked. The footsteps move away. He lowers the board, his breath catching. Tossing the board aside he walks to the back of the dark basement. His prey is still asleep, it was taking a long time for him to wake up.

He has his weapon ready, ready for when his prey wakes up, ready for justice, ready to show the evil one that he couldn't have his pretty, she was his conquest, his prize, he was the one meant to spend eternity with her. And what justice to take his lifeblood at the demon's house.

His prey moves, groans, the eyes open slowly, they look around the room, they settle on me. He sees confusion then anger in his dark eyes, he sees fury, he is full of evil. It will be a pleasure to destroy the evil one.

He raises his weapon, ready to strike the first blow, ready to end his reign. As he starts to lower his weapon the evil one rolls away. He screams. The evil one is on his feet, his hands and ankles are free, how did he get released from his bindings? He is evil, he possesses power. But not for long. He swings his weapon again hoping to slice the stomach of the evil one. The evil one jumps away but catches his foot on a loose rock and falls, his head bounces as he lands. His eyes close.

He kicks his prey again and again trying to wake him up, he has to be awake, he has to watch as his life is taken away.

He sits and waits for the evil one to open his eyes again. While he waits he thinks of the smile that will be on his pretty's face when she finds out that he took the evil one away. When she discovers how powerful he is, he has taken many lords away, he has taken the women that made the lords happy, she will be pleased with me, she will be ready to be my soul mate. We will spend our live together in her kingdom, free of lords that think they wield power.

He kicks his prey again, this time he moans. Standing over him, he waits for the eyes to open, to see the dark menace in those eyes. He was waiting but suddenly his prey swings his legs, knocking him to the floor. He swings his weapon as his prey gets to his feet, it connects on the man's thigh. He is rewarded with the sight of blood. The beginning of the end for the evil one.

He staggers to his feet, his prey leaning on the wall behind him. He walks to his prey, he smiles, now was the time. But his prey raises his hands, a long board in his hands, he swings it at the weapon trying to knock it from the hands that held it, it falls to the ground, the man screams before charging at him, they fight until they were both gasping for breath.

He screams, his prey backs up a step, he reaches down and picks his weapon up just as his prey charges him, this time the end of the blade slices through his side. He screams. He raises his *weapon ready for the final blow but a noise stops him. What is that grinding? What is that beating? Why is it making his head hurt? He takes another swing at his prey this time slicing through his stomach again. He screams before falling to the ground holding his hands over his ears before he loses consciousness. His prey falling at his side.*

><

Ron and I meet the detective in the church hallway, thankfully it wasn't John Green. As Ron fills the detective in on what had happened and the worry that our suspect may have something to do with Wade's disappearance, I go back into the office to check on Ann. She seems to have regrouped as the officers talk to her, giving her a smile I leave the office.

While Ron talks I head for the sanctuary thinking a little prayer time was in order. Entering the large cavernous room, my heart fills. I take a seat in one of the front pews, closing my eyes letting my mind go blank, focusing on Jesus instead of the demon. The sound of the organ slowly starts filling the room with a poignant sound, almost soul wrenching. Sitting quietly while they play, letting the music wash over me, as the music gets louder the calm my soul was feeling now takes over. I close my eyes again knowing that the Lord was giving me peace, He was giving me strength, He was giving me the calm I needed.

Quietly I get up hoping to not disturb the organist as she practices, shutting the door softly behind me and with a new determination. Wade was going to be found and alive. No psychotic demon was going to win this battle.

Rejoining Ron in the hallway as the officers were checking the premises, their conclusion was the same as ours. They didn't think any foul play had been involved, but with no idea where Wade had gone to. They were heading to canvass the area, checking local businesses and stores thinking they may have seen something.

One officer had the thought maybe he hit his head some way and was confused now, maybe walking off and didn't know his way back. But there was no evidence of any type of injury, no blood, no impressions in the grass that he may have fallen. And I wasn't buying that, I knew that Hanzor had him, just not where he had him.

After the last officer leaves with a promise from the detective that he was leaving one here in a car out front, I think what good would that do but don't say anything.

When the door shuts behind the detective Ron looks at me. "Ready to search the whole place? I'm sure there are dozens of hiding places here."

With a sigh of relief. "Thank you. Let's start at the top, the bell tower."

Letting Ann know what we were going to do, she hands me a key. "I'll lock everything but the back door. We've cancelled all the activities for the day so you have the place to yourselves."

Thanking her we head for the gigantic staircase that went all the way to the top of the church and the bell tower. Standing at the bottom, Ron looks up. "How many floors?"

"Six. What you out of shape? Sorry but there isn't an elevator in the church."

"Great."

We make our way to the last step, in front of us was an intricately engraved wooden door. "This is it, the end of the stairs and the entrance to the bell tower. Prepared to be impressed."

Opening the door we step into the chamber, the bell hung in the middle, a black wrought iron bell, worn from decades of weather. A metal catwalk surrounded the bell, large enough that three people could walk abreast around the entire chamber. All four sides were open to the most spectacular view of Boston and the area.

Standing at the opening with the view of the harbor, I take in the scenery mentally asking where Wade could be. I look to the left where you could see most of the warehouse district. Was he in one of those empty buildings? It would take months to go through each one. Where would Hanzor take him and did he have him? So many questions.

We spend the rest of the day going through the whole church, and I mean every single inch. Back on the first floor I sit down on one of the stairs while Ron sits down in one of the ornate chairs that were positioned every few feet in small groupings. "So the only place we haven't looked is the basement, but it's locked."

Clapping his hands on his knees. "Let's go eat. Neither one of us have eaten all day, we'll both think better once we have some food." Standing he motions for me to come on.

Leaving by the back door, I make sure to lock it behind us before we head for the closest diner.

><

He rises slowly, shaking his head, trying to clear the distorted images. He was seeing his prey sitting on the floor across from him, he was smiling. The evil one thinks he has won this battle. He picks his weapon up, why did the evil one leave it for him to have? The evil one gets up too, puts a hand out. What does he want? Raising my weapon, he screams as he charges at his prey, the weapon slices through the air, his prey steps away at the last second, he pulls his hand back landing a painful punch. The evil one pulls his hand back again, landing another painful punch this time to the face. He staggers back, he raises his weapon he

217

screams as he runs toward his prey, the weapon buries itself in his side, the prey moans as he pulls the weapon out. He screams. Almost, he has his prey almost. His pretty will be so pleased. The prey hasn't fallen to the ground in defeat instead he takes a step forward hitting him again and again. The weapon falls to the ground as he falls the scream never leaving his mouth.

><

They eat in silence, Grace's mind couldn't focus on anything but Wade and where he was. Ron knew how worried she was but for her to maneuver through the day she needed to eat instead of picking at her food.

"Grace. Eat. Now."

Knowing Ron was right I finally manage to get the sandwich down and the glass of tea. Wiping my hands before laying my napkin on my plate. "Let's go break into the basement."

"So you really think there's something down there?"

"Probably not, but I won't rest until I know for sure."

Ron wipes his hands before laying a few bills on the table with what Grace has put down. "We need some kind of crowbar to pry that door open with."

I think of the small hardware store one block down. "I know where to get one."

Once we had the crowbar we head back to the church. Walking around the building to the back we both stop in our tracks. The basement door was open.

Chapter 26

Both of us frozen in our tracks before I notice the trail of blood. "Ron the blood."

He nods as he takes the lead, pulling his weapon he leads the way into the dark basement. His flashlight cuts through the darkness of the dank room. The trail of blood leads from the back of the basement, following with Grace behind they follow the trail to a large cavernous empty room. "There's been a fight in here."

There was blood in several different places, on the floor and the walls. But no bodies and no Wade.

Ron squats down, running his finger through the blood. "This is fresh."

"We haven't been gone more than an hour." I run my hands through my hair.

Standing up Ron wraps an arm around Grace. "We'll find him, there's no way a body could be carried out of here without someone seeing something." Squeezing her a little. "Yes there's a lot of blood but not enough to that someone is dead. And this could be from both of them."

I nod trying to understand. I needed to get into the demons mind again. Walking to the center of the room, I close my eyes imagining the fight between the lord and the knight. Wade was strong and powerful, besides running he works out several days a week. Hanzor depends on his weapon. I picture them fighting, I see Hanzor swinging his knife, maybe slicing Wade but not imbedding his weapon. I see Wade punching him, again and again. I see Wade stumbling, holding his side. Opening my eyes. Hoping that what I imagined was true, that Wade got away.

Ron was on his phone when I turn back around, undoubtedly reporting what we found. I could hear the captain yelling from where I was standing.

But I couldn't stand here and wait for the techs so I start following the trail of blood. When I get to the top of the basement steps I stomp my foot, while we were in the basement night had fallen.

Joining me Ron curses under his breath. "We
can't wait until morning the trail may be gone by
then."

"Let's get some flashlights then we'll each
take a trail maybe we can find something."

"Good idea but where are we going to find
flashlights?"

"Wade's always prepared and the power goes off
in this old building all the time." I lead the way
to the back door unlocking it then we head for
Wade's office. Opening the closet in his office to
find enough supplies to stock a small store. We
each grab a large flashlight then head back
outside.

Automatically I take the left and Ron heads to
the right as more lights come around the side of
the building. A few officers were followed by a
couple of techs. As Ron talks to them I shine my
beam on the trail of blood following it to the back
of the lot. The trail goes over the fence, so I
jump it picking the trail up on the other side.
Unfortunately the lot was overgrown with weeds,
filled with trash and debris. The trail stops right

before the lot meets the sidewalk. Shining my light on the ground, searching for the trail, but it just stopped. Oh Lord, help me!

Crisscrossing the lot not once but twice I don't find anymore blood.

Retracing my steps to the fence, jumping back across to see Ron doing his own crisscrossing in the back yard. Meeting him in the middle. "Any luck?"

"No. Trail ends at the edge. You?"

"Trail ends at the sidewalk." Talk about feeling defeated. We walk slowly back to the building to find the techs were busy taking pictures and tagging whatever they could. An officer approaches us holding a plastic bag.

"Detective we found this in the corner." He holds the bag and I grab it when I see what was inside.

"This is Wade's cross. He never took it off." Studying the cross I notice that the chain was broken so it had been pulled off his neck. And that made sense since this whole thing was based on

223

evil. Handing the bag back to the officer he nods at me before turning back to work.

Ron grabs my arm. "Come on, we need to leave. There's nothing more we can do here. Go home try to get some rest and we'll start again in the morning." He motions for an officer. "Make sure she gets home and don't drop her off anywhere else no matter how much she complains." He gives my address to the officer probably to make sure I didn't give a fake one so I could walk the streets.

><

He walks in the shadows stumbling every few feet, the evil one had hurt him bad. He couldn't take a breath, he couldn't stand up straight. He needed to get to a safe place to rest then once he was strong again he would hunt again. He screams. The evil one got away, he's strong, too strong with evil, he would spread that evil around even to my pretty, he needed to be stopped. Anger boils in his blood, he needed a killing, he needed a sacrifice. He needed blood on his hands. He pulls the knife from the sheath on his back, he looks around, he sees a young woman walking to him, he screams as he slices her neck open, he puts his hand in the blood as it pours from the wound, he rubs the blood on his face, he runs to hide.

><

Letting Grace out in front of her building she thanks the officer before getting out. He sits and waits as she unlocks the door and enters her building and still sits. Climbing the stairs she enters her apartment, going through her routine before shutting her door.

Pulling her jacket off she kicks her shoes across the room before going into the kitchen to make a fresh pot of coffee, it was going to be a long night.

Chapter 27

After three mugs of coffee and absolutely no way that sleep was going to come, I give up and start to put my shoes on. Hearing my phone ringing, I reach into my jacket pocket. It was Ron. "Shouldn't you be trying to get some sleep?"

His voice was hoarse. "We have him. Wade. A passerby found him unconscious behind Jetto's market. He's in surgery now, there's a car out front waiting for you." He hangs up.

With one shoe on and carrying the other I slam out of my apartment, running down the stairs. Ripping the front door open to find the captain sitting in a car at the curb. Climbing in the passenger seat I turn to him. "Tell me."

As he starts the car and I get my other shoe on. "One of the busboys at Jetto's was taking the trash out and found Wade crumpled against the wall. He called his boss out and he recognized him, they called it in. Wade is in surgery, he has three deep

gashes across his stomach one perforated his side.
It sliced a kidney and they're trying now to repair
it, if not he can manage fine on one. He also has a
broken cheek bone and a broken hand. From his
wounds I'd say the other guy is in pretty bad shape
so it may just be a matter of time before he shows
up, dead."

Stopping at the entrance to the hospital I
jump out while the captain parks. At the admissions
desk I tell the orderly that was on duty who I was
and who I was inquiring about. "He's still in
surgery, the waiting room is on the third floor."

Taking off for the stairs instead of waiting
for the elevator I reach the waiting room to see
Ron and two other officers waiting. Joining Ron.
"Any news?"

Shaking his head. "Not yet, but it looks
good." He had bags under his eyes, his voice was
hoarse and I was sure I didn't look much better.
"We have another murder. This one right on
Congress. Whoever it was walked up to Megan
Summers, sliced her throat open and left. I'd say
he's past escalation, he's on a rampage now."

Closing my eyes, I say a prayer for the victim adding healing for Wade and help with finding this guy. It was personal now. Slouching back in my chair to wait and think.

Ron leans his head back against the wall. "They have the whole area cordoned off and are doing a building by building search."

"Won't find him."

"I know but they need to try." He closes his eyes desperately in need of sleep.

"Why don't you go home and rest. I'll let you know if anything changes."

"Can't."

"Why?"

Opening his eyes he turns to me. "Because that demon is in my head and I can't sleep."

"I'm sorry Ron, I really am. I'll suggest to the captain not to put you with me anymore."

"Oh no you don't." Leaning closer to me lowering his voice. "I always thought being a detective was the best thing to be, catching the bad guy, investigating, catching the ones that were covering up crimes until I started working with you. You made me realize what evil there is out there, that the people I was dealing with were nothing compared to what you saw. Yes I've lost some sleep, yes I've had nightmares, I've let what you call the demons take over. I've tried to put myself in their shoes like you do, I can't but I will. And once we get this guy I know those demons will go away that we got evil off the street until the next one comes. But you are not telling the captain I can't handle it. I plan on being beside you on the next one and the next one. I feel as if I'm actually alive now and you are not taking that away." With a slight glare at me, he closes his eyes, leaning his head against the wall again. "Now shut up and let me see if I can catch a few." A smile crosses his face.

A smile crosses my face too as I take his hand and squeeze. Well it appears I have a partner now. Who would have thought?

Waiting was never a strong point with and especially since I was waiting to hear about someone I cared deeply about. I pick up a magazine and flip through before tossing is back down. I pull my cell phone out, checking for any messages and looking at the news. Turning my attention to the TV, the sound was muted but the captions were running across the bottom of the screen. The murder tonight was the main story, oh my gosh Megan had only been 16. Closing my eyes, I start talking in my head to God, asking him to help point me in the direction I needed to go, to be with Wade and the families of the ones that had been killed. I pour my heart out not realizing that tears were running down my face until I feel a finger on my cheek.

Opening my eyes to see Ron wiping my tears away. I give him a smile as a door across the hall opens and a doctor walks out. I stand as he approaches us, Ron stands beside me.

"Ms. Hanson?"

"Yes."

"Mr. Caufrey came through the surgery just fine. We have him in an induced coma right now and will keep him like that for at least another day because of the damage from the broken cheekbone. But his prognosis is good, very good. Now may I suggest you all go home and get some rest." He starts to turn away.

"Doctor can I just see him for a minute?" I clasp my hands together to keep from grabbing the lapel of his coat.

Looking at me before smiling. "Just for a minute. He's asleep but I can tell you need to see for yourself." He gestures for me to follow him.

Once he leads me to the bed in recovery that Wade was in, he says softly. "Two minutes."

Nodding at him I turn my attention to Wade. His face was badly bruised, his cheek swollen to three times its normal size, both eyes were black and swollen, there were several cuts on his chin and other cheek. His hand was in a cast and bandages covered his torso. Tubes and wires were hooked everywhere. Carefully taking his uninjured hand I squeeze it. "I'm here Wade and you're going to be all right. You're in the best hands ever." I lean forward and kiss his cheek. "I do love you."

Knowing I wouldn't get a response, I squeeze his hand one more time before leaving.

Returning to the waiting room to find the officers had left and Ron was sipping from a cup of coffee with another sitting on the table in front of him. Seeing me he gets up. "Well?"

Letting a breath out as I run my hand through my hair. "Badly bruised, cuts, lacerations, hand in a cast his torso covered in bandages, but he'll be fine. He'll make it." Smiling as I pick the cup of coffee up, turning my eyes back to him. "Ready?"

Downing the last of his coffee he dunks it in the trash can. "Let's go kick some butt."

Chapter 28

Grabbing a cab in the front of the hospital, I tell Ron. "I need a shower and change of clothes. How about we meet where Megan was in two hours."

"Works for me." His phone pings. Pulling it from his pocket he reads the text then smiles. "It's from the captain, he's says do whatever we have to, he's sitting on the mayor."

"Hum. Carte Blanche, that's a new one. Think he'd believe it if we said we had a lead that's taking us to the Caribbean?"

With a snort. "Doubtful."

The cab stops in front of my apartment building, I look at my watch. "Two hours." He nods while I give the cabbie my share of the fare. As I get out and the cab pulls away, I feel that creepy feeling again. Turning around I look hard at everyone on the street, but it was all normal as usual.

Once I was in my apartment, I skip the ritual heading for the window instead. Looking at the building across the street but it was just a building nothing sinister about it in the bright sunlight.

After a shower and fresh clothes I was ready to conquer the world or catch a demon. Pulling on boots, an extra sweater and a clean jacket, I tuck everything I may need in my pockets thinking of all the files I usually carry with a smile, this was so much easier.

Checking the time, I still had an hour so I go into the kitchen to make a pot of coffee. While it was brewing, I sit at the kitchen table and think. If I were the killer and had been hurt where would I go? Not the hospital or a doctor. The place where he conducted the rituals was not an option now, so where was his hang out? Where did he go to sleep, to plan his rituals? It had to be another vacant building but there were hundreds in the city. But everything had happened in the south end. So how many vacant buildings, maybe twenty or thirty? It was worth a try.

Downing a cup of coffee before sipping the next cup. Maybe if we concentrated in the areas closest to where the victims were found. That would take the count down to maybe ten. Still worth a try.

Setting my cup in the sink I slip my jacket on then leave the apartment, locking the door behind me, I head for the front door, making sure it was locked behind me.

Walking to Congress Street taking a little longer than normal since it was lunchtime and the sidewalks were packed, I finally reach the area where Megan had been killed to find Ron already there. He was talking to a woman that was holding the leash of a small dog that was yipping it's head off and pulling on the leash.

As I approach my eyes stay on the dog, it was trying to get to something beside the trash container. Waving to Ron I lean down to look under the container seeing something shiny. Slipping my hand underneath I grasp the tiny object, pulling my hand out to find an earring, it must have been

Megan's. He definitely hit her with some force to pull an earring loose.

Ron finishes his conversation with the woman. "What's that?"

"Must be from Megan." Looking at Ron. "Find anything out?"

"Only that the people that live around here are scared and don't think the police are doing enough."

"I hope you straightened her out."

"I did. So question the businesses? She was killed a little after 6am."

"Then not many businesses would have been open." My eyes land on the coffee shop across the street. "But maybe that coffee shop."

We cross the street to find a small line inside the shop, waiting our turn I take advantage of ordering a coffee before asking for the manager. Sipping the coffee as we wait I stand in front of the window noticing several cameras were in the area, hopefully some officers already had the video.

"Can I help you?" A tall young man with light red hair and blue eyes with a winning smile walks towards us.

Ron shows his badge and asks the young man. "Good morning, we were wondering if by chance you or any of your employees noticed anything this morning, anything suspicious, anything out of the ordinary."

The smile disappears from the young man's face. "It's about Megan isn't it?"

"You knew her?" I ask.

He nods, swallowing hard. "She works um worked here part time."

"Were you here this morning?" Ron was being gentle.

"No. I didn't get here until a little after 8am but I've talked to everybody that was here and no one saw or heard anything. I wish I could help more, Megan didn't deserve that."

"We know that she didn't. If by chance you talk to anyone that did see something can you give us a call?" Ron hands the young man his card. With a nod he walks off and we leave the shop.

"I have a feeling we're not going to find anyone that saw anything." Ron plants his hands on his hips.

Looking around at the activity, the businesses, the shops, my eye catches a man sitting in the doorway of a loan office. He was watching me. Taking a chance I head over to him, squatting in front of him. Looking into his eyes I could see intelligence there. "Did you see something this morning?"

He nods.

"Would you like to share? I want to catch this guy. Badly. He hurt a friend of mine too."

He nods then points behind me and shakes his head. Turning to see what was behind me, Ron. "You can just talk to me, I'll tell him to go away." The man gives me a crooked smile as I turn to motion Rom to walk away. "I've only taken a sip of this coffee would you like the rest?"

Holding both hands out, I hand him the coffee. He takes a sip before smiling again. Clearing his throat. "I was here when that monster attacked Megan, it took everything for me to not run after him. He was about your height, slim, wearing a dark hoodie covered in stains. Appeared to have dark hair and a couple of days' worth of stubble. He pushed his hood off and pulled the knife from his collar area." He demonstrated how the knife was pulled out. "He screamed then lunged at the girl with a sideways arc, she didn't have a chance. As she fell he screamed again before running east toward the business district. He also held his side a little as he ran off."

I plop down on my butt, the man's speech was impeccable, he was highly intelligent as his eyes revealed so why was he sitting on the doorstep of a closed business in clothes that were so dirty and old they would probably disintegrate if washed. The look on my face must have told exactly what I was thinking.

The man actually giggles. "I know. I'm a little undercover also. I'm actually a professor of economic culture at Boston University and am doing a little research. I suppose I've really gotten into my disguise though from the look on your face." Holding a hand out to me. "Edgar Reynolds."

Taking his hand. "Grace Hanson, I work with the Boston PD."

"And this is a rough one. This is connected to the other killings?"

Nodding my head. "Yes we think so."

"I will certainly keep my eyes open then. Do you have a card with your number on it and I can relay any information."

Handing him my card. "Thank you Mr. Reynolds, you've been a big help."

With a regal nod of his head I get up and rejoin Ron who was leaning against a lamp post. "Did he see anything?"

"Yes he saw the whole thing. Described our perp down to holding his side when he ran and running east toward the business district."

"Then let's start walking."

Chapter 29

We walk for what seems like forever, stopping every couple of blocks describing the man we were looking for. Inspecting vacant buildings, checking alleyways, looking for anything. Finally we both stop, leaning against the building across the street from my apartment.

"Let's call it a day. Have you checked on Wade today?"

"Yes they still have him in a coma but are going to bring him out tomorrow. Everything else looks really good."

"Good. So what do we work on tomorrow?" Ron holds a hand over a yawn.

"Let's see if tonight's quiet then I have an idea on what area he may be using. We'll start there tomorrow." Stifling my own yawn.

"Good night Grace. Sweet dreams." He waves as he walks toward the station.

Crossing the street to my building, I unlock the front door, collect my mail then wearily climb the stairs to my floor. The TV was on in the opposite apartment. I unlock my door, go through my little ritual then shut and lock my door. Crossing the room without turning any lights on, I look out over what part of the city I can see including the building next door. "Lord help us find this creature. Help us capture him and stop the senseless killings and please continue to heal Wade."

Taking a long hot shower then climbing into comfortable sweats, I fix a cup of tea before crawling onto the couch. I knew I should be digging more into the actions of this guy but right now I just needed to get my head away from him before he takes over completely.

><

He watches as she and that man walk up and down the street. What are they looking for? Did she lose a pet or something? He knows the man she's with is a policeman and he will be dealt with later for being close to her instead of the one that should be.

He saw the police pick up the dead girl this morning and he knew the other man was probably dead in the alley he saw him fall himself.

He opens the door to the building making sure no one sees him. He takes the stairs to the bottom floor making sure all the doors shut behind him. He goes to the back of the building opening the last door. He shuts it behinds him. He walks to the corner of the room and lies down. He must rest before he tries to capture his pretty, it's time. He has proved his worth, he has killed for her, he has presented her presents and now she must know. She has been won from the evil one. She is his. He will claim his pretty soon.

><

After watching a little TV, I crawl into my bed pulling the blankets up to my chin. Closing my eyes I ask the Lord for a good night's sleep so that my mind will be clear tomorrow. This can't go on any longer.

Jerking awake from a horrible dream, I sit for a minute, sweat trickling down my back. And it was a really horrible dream, one where Wade hadn't made it. Knowing sleep was going to be impossible now, I get up for that cup of coffee.

As I wait for the coffee to brew, I go to the window. "Where are you Hanzor? Where?" Not really looking at anything my eyes fall to the building across the street and the top floor. Now I know I just had a really bad dream and my mind may not be in the best place but that is a flashlight moving around. Tossing some clothes on, filling my pockets I flip the coffee off before leaving my apartment. At the front door I stand and watch the light for a few minutes just to make sure I wasn't seeing things before I open the door.

Crossing the street I approach the building, at one time it was an insurance company then a printing company before it was shuttered. Pulling the door open to total darkness except for the little ribbons of light from the street lights that was coming through the grimy windows, I stand and wait for my eyes to adjust.

Now how to get to the top floor? The bottom floor was open to falling and toppled cubicles, the whole room open except for a few offices on the side walls. As quietly as I can I walk through the center of the room listening. Reaching the back of the room to find several doors, now which one led to the stairway? Taking my flashlight out I shine it on the floor finding footprints leading under the third door.

Pushing the door open to find another cavernous room, only this time it was empty. Shining my light around the room the far wall catches my attention. Walking over I stand in front of the wall shining my light on pieces of paper with ramblings written every which way. Everything from my pretty, my beloved, conquest, kill the lords, the knights rule, and then the list of names, names of the people he's killed except the last three are the boy in the alley, the woman on the street, the evil one from rock building and then the little girl. On My Lord.

Running my eyes back up the list, the first six that we found are there along with five other names. So there are more out there that we haven't found or they could have been in those barrels.

My stomach churns at the thought that we may never know which name belongs to which body. He has to be stopped.

Turning my light back to the room, there are two more doors on the back wall, following the footprints in the dust to the door I knew I was supposed to use.

Taking a deep breath I open the door, it opens to a stairwell that leads up. Okay.

Shining my light up the stairs, they're steep and made of metal so I take my time ascending. At the first landing I shine my light on the floor, no footprints going under the doorway so I continue to the next landing where there are two doors, one on the right, one on the left and both seem have been used judging by the footprints in the dust. Taking the door on the left first I open to find myself on the roof.

I follow the footprints to where they stop at the edge with a direct line of sight into my apartment. So I wasn't imagining the creepy feeling, he had been watching me.

Chapter 30

Anger starts to surface, my fists clinch into tight balls. I wanted to hit something instead I close my eyes and try to refocus my anger on something else, picturing the face of Jesus in my head I feel the anger ebbing away.

Shaking my shoulders I turn back to the door, I was going to face this monster head on. Making sure the door didn't slam behind me as I reenter the building, I look at the other door. This must be the room that he uses as living quarters. Pushing open the door the welcome sight of light from the streetlamps coming in is a relief. Lowering my flashlight, the room was empty except the walls were covered in drawings. Drawings of lords and knights fighting, of the distant wall with the conquest standing alone, her dark hair and dress blowing in the breeze. Dead bodies with swords protruding from their bodies were lying on the ground that was painted a bright red. Yellow eyes look out from the trees and bushes that had been painted in clumps. On one wall an altar was painted with a man lying on it, blood pouring from his body with the knight standing over him, his hood covering his face, his arms were raised over his head ready to bring down the sword again. Behind the altar a ghostly figure stood, a woman wearing a long white dress, her long hair blowing in each direction, but she has no face, her arms were outstretched as if welcoming you into a hug.

This person was past being psychotic, as Ron said he was just plain crazy and I don't think any amount of psychology would help. If we do catch him alive he'll be locked into a mental facility the rest of his life with absolutely no chance of release if I have to give my recommendation.

Having enough of the ghastly scenery, I retrace my steps to the door. Taking the stairs to the second floor, I really don't think he'll be there, he'd want a place dark and dank where he can be himself in the darkness where no one can see him so I bypass the landing, continuing on to the first floor in search of the basement door.

Reentering the first floor I try another door in search of the basement. The third door that was in the corner opened to stairs leading down into total darkness.

Clicking my flashlight on I descend expecting the worse at the bottom. Instead I find two more doors, shining my light on the floor I put my hand on the handle of the door with footprints underneath. The door squeaks just a bit as I open it.

Total darkness greets me along with a smell that I recognize from the ZoneRoom. This is where he stays. Sweeping my light around the room slowly, hopefully not to be surprised by anything. There are mounds of clothing or rags all over the floor along with old food wrappers, crumpled cups and newspapers. An old refrigerator sits in one corner along with a rickety table with a chair. In the farthest corner is a discarded mattress that seems covered in clothes or blankets and standing at the head of that bed is Hanzor.

I can only make out the shape of a man of medium height who is slim but not skinny. He's wearing dark clothes with the hood from his jacket covering his face. My fear level jumps, making my heart beat against my chest. But I couldn't show him my fear.

Taking a step closer, my light moving away from his face to his hands which were clasped in front of him.

He takes a step forward with a slight growl. I decide he isn't aware of who I am so I swing the light to my face and watch as he visibly relaxes.

"My pretty." The voice is rough, gravelly and low.

"Yes."

"You came."

"Yes."

"You've seen my presents, my gifts, my redemption for your grace."

"No." Turning the light away from my face before taking a step closer.

"What do I call you? My name is Grace."

"No you are My Pretty and that is what you will be called." His head bows a little. "I have no name worthy of you but you can call me Hanzor."

"Hanzor. I know that you conquered many adversaries, many lords. I know you also killed many innocent people like the young girl from yesterday." I was hoping to get him in a weakened mental state.

His hands slowly rise as he shakes them. "No one is innocent. No one except you. You are pure. You are precious."

Taking a gamble. "Do you really know who I am?"

"Yes. My pretty."

"I work for the Boston Police Department. I'm a profiler hired to figure out the minds of people like you. People that kill or maim for no reason. Why did you kill that young boy in the alley and the young girl last night? They weren't the enemy, they hadn't lived long enough to be evil."

With a whimper he swings an arm around. "They needed to be sacrifices for my anger."

Standing my ground. "Your anger doesn't deserve a sacrifice."

He screams. A bloodcurdling, full of hate scream. He takes a few steps toward me, the odor intensifying with his approach. "The blood I spill is for your grace."

"No. I don't need an innocent's spilt blood, I have the grace of God."

Standing stock still, I have a glimmer of hope that maybe that got through a little but I was wrong, the next scream is even louder than the last one and this one beings him charging in my direction. I swing the light to my face, it makes him stop short. He stares at me, his face still in shadows. "NO!" He screams even louder, this time beating his head with his fists. "NO!" He swings around with his fist connecting with my jaw.

My face whips to the left, hard, the punch he gives me sending waves of pain through my jaw. Slowly turning my head to face him again, I move my jaw a little to make sure he hadn't broken it. His hood has fallen away from his face. His eyes were black, the scar at his left eyebrow and chin dominate his face, his nose has been broken a few times, the stubble on his cheek and chin dark. Under different circumstances the man would be consider handsome.

"You are an impostor! You are not my pretty." He spits at my feet before slamming himself into the wall behind him.

"Why do you say that? You've been watching me, you've made sacrifices for me."

"Your eyes they are evil."

Then I remembered all his victims had dark hair and eyes. I have dark hair and light green eyes. In his mind I was an enemy. And I was going to pay for that.

Chapter 31

He starts pacing, back and forth mumbling to himself. He didn't know what to do.

"Come with me. I can get you help."

"No! You will destroy me! I need my pretty I cannot exist without her." He yells at me as he rips his jacket off exposing a blood stained shirt. He charges again, this time he ducks before hitting me full force, we both fall to the concrete floor. With him lying on top of me, he grabs a fistful of my hair in both hands.

I stare at him, not moving, letting him get the confidence that I'm not a threat. He screams in my face which made me cringe from the odor. Twisting my head as he lets go of my hair, I let go of the breath I had been holding. Slowly I get up, never taking my eyes off him. He leans against the far wall his head ducked just a little but I knew he was watching every move I made. Knowing that nothing I say will change his mind about giving up and coming with me, I start thinking of ways to get out of here now. Just walking to the door and leaving probably wasn't going to be an option, but I was going to try.

Leaning down I pick up my flashlight that had fallen from my hand when he hit me, I turn it back on with a sad look at him. Lowering my eyes I turn and start for the door. Before I've taken two steps he has me in a death grip around my waist, picking me up slinging me to the mattress, I land with a thump before bouncing once.

Sitting up he gives me what I think is a smile but was more a grimace. Kicking some of the debris that littered the place he finds some zip ties. I back up a little then try to get my feet under me to move but he was quicker than I was, pulling me back by my hair again. Sitting on me he roughly pulls my wrists together before zip tying them together, he did the same with my ankles. Satisfied that I was now bound and couldn't get loose he picks his hoodie up, sliding his arms in he smiles at me. "I will be back to finish this."

He slams from the room then I hear a soft click, he's locked me in this dark, dank, smelly room and who knew how long it will be before he's back. But. He didn't take any of the goodies I have stuffed in my pockets.

Since he zip tied my hands in front of me I reach into my left pocket as carefully as I can, pulling my pocket knife out. Slicing the zip ties around my wrist off I move to my ankles, tossing the ties to the side I reach back into my pocket for my cell phone. Of course no bars. Walking around the room holding my phone to the ceiling, toward the wall and at the door, nothing.

Okay think Grace. Using the flashlight app on the phone, I take in the room, trying to remember everything before tapping my phone to save the battery. With my hands in front of me, I make my way to the refrigerator pulling the door open. Mostly to see if there is electricity rather than food. Yuck, even if I was hungry whatever was inside was rotten, and it wasn't cold. So no power.

Sitting down on the one rickety chair in the room, I think of how I can overpower him. I had a set of handcuffs but didn't even think to bring my weapon with me, now how smart was that.

Tapping my phone again I shine the light down each wall looking for anything, a hook, pipes, electrical wires, anything, but this room was bare.

Kicking through the debris on the floor, dirty clothes, oily rags, trash and old food, nothing I can use as a weapon.

Plopping back down on the nasty mattress wondering how long he was going to leave me down here. With the way his mind works it could be days before he decides to see if he really did see me down here or it was a figment of his imagination. But I needed to be ready so I fall back on the mattress thinking a nap would be good if I needed to fight but knowing I most likely wouldn't fall asleep.

This wasn't working I couldn't lay here just waiting. Getting up, I start pacing a little trying to make a plan. If I stand beside the door when he opens it, I could surprise him then maybe get the cuffs on him before he has a chance to react.

I start clearing things away from beside the door, feeling my way in the dark was a little nerve-racking but I kept pushing on. On my hands and knees I feel the floor, I had everything cleared away.

With my hands in front of me to keep me from bumping into a wall, I make my way to the other side of the room where I slide the table to the far corner along with the chair. As flimsy as they both were it may not hurt to fall on one but broken slivers of wood could be dangerous.

That was about all I could do for now. Oh for a cup of coffee. I was getting antsy, my nerves were jumpy I needed to do something so I start hopping in place, then change to jumping jacks before dropping to the floor to do a few planks. Taking a few minutes of rest I resume hopping hoping to burn some of this nervous energy up. Let's get this over with!

How long has he been gone, an hour, two? More likely ten minutes. Knowing there was no way possible to sleep I start running my hands over the wall farthest from the door. Maybe there was a boarded up window or an entry to another room. But nothing.

Pressing my back to the wall I walk straight, counting each step until my hands touch the door, forty two steps. So I start walking back and forth from the door to the wall, back and forth, back and forth. I stopped after thirty times. Then I ball my hands into fists and do some air punches, imaging him standing in front of me.

By now my muscles were loose and limber, ready. But where the devil did he go and was he coming back? Walking back to the door feeling for the hinges, there were three, now if I only had something to work the bolts out. Feeling around the refrigerator and in the small cabinet but nothing was sharp enough or strong enough.

Going back to the mattress I sit where my back was against the wall weighing my options, which were few. Pulling the almost flat pillow to tuck behind my back I feel something hard. Running my hand over the mattress my fingers curl around a long hard object, picking it up it feels a little sticky but it was a knife or rather a machete. The murder weapon? Lifting the knife in my hands, it was sharp and it was heavy but the weight was in the hilt, a good weapon to swing with force, no wonder he could cut the throat so deeply with one slice.

Getting off the bed, I swing the machete around, getting used to the feel, the weight, the way the blade whistled as it cut through the air.

How ironic would it be to use his own weapon on him?

Chapter 32

How long has he been gone? It feels like days. I needed to get some rest some way so I try to lay down again, keeping the machete close and getting used to the odor in the room, it wasn't so bad now. Closing my eyes I turn all my thoughts to Jesus, pouring out my frustrations and my fears before praying.

My eyes pop open taking a second to remember where I was. Wonder how long I had been asleep and how long I've been down here now?

Getting up I do a few deep knee bends then stretch my arms up and over my head. Reaching on the bed for the machete I tuck it into the back of my belt, ready.

Resuming my walk back and forth between the door and the wall adding a few lunges in every few steps. If nothing else as tight as my nerves were waiting for him to return, I'll be able to put up a good fight.

Thinking back over the few things he'd said before he left. He couldn't rationalize reality from the game, so he was delusional, could I use that to my advantage? He also had a predisposed image of what a conquest was and that wasn't going to change.

><

He walks, and walks, his pretty, his pretty. All the sacrifices he had made were for nothing. Nothing. Stuffing his hands in the pockets of his hoodie, his head hanging low. What to do? Go back and dismiss her? Go back and make her a gift for the conquest when he does find her? He leans against the wall in an alley. He felt let down, he felt cheated, he felt like he had been tricked. He needed to feel alive again. Take another gift? Raising his head to watch the people pass the alley. Does he dare take another sacrifice? For what? His pretty? Slowly anger builds, she tricked him! She made him believe she was the prize and all along she was on the opposite side! He screams before turning to the end of the alley, he starts to reach out to grab a body as he reaches to his

back then stops, dropping his hands. His weapon,

she had his weapon, he couldn't take another gift.

She had tricked him again. She must pay. He walks,

he walks more until he lays down to sleep. When he

was rested he would go back and give her what she

deserved.

><

How could she convince him, pretend they were

in the game? She didn't know enough about it to

play, but maybe she could bluff her way. Thinking a

conquest was like a queen. And a queen was royalty,

a queen would look down on her people. Feeling

around the edge of the walls, looking for something

to stand on, something that would make her taller

than him so that he had to look up to her. But the

only thing she could find was the discarded clothes

and rags. Maybe if she piled them up enough it

would appear that she was on a pedestal of sort.

Crawling on the floor she pushed all of the rags

and clothes into a pile against the wall facing the

door, laying as many as possible flat so they

wouldn't sink when she stood on them. Using everything she found on the floor she made her own little stage. Standing on her improvised stage, if she balanced herself this would work, she'd be at least a few inches taller than him. With that done, she crawled on the floor some more to see what else she could use, but the most she found were a few rotten pieces of food and trash. Leaning on the wall beside the door, what else could she do to make him think she was still the conquest? A cape? Crawling to the bed she pulls the top blanket off, tying two ends around her neck, it was long but it would work. Now to wait and that was the hard part.

Pulling my cell out again trying to see if by chance there were any bars, but no still nothing. Using the flashlight for just a second, I sweep the light around the room and smile, moving all the clothing to one pile had improved the place immensely.

Clicking my phone off, I tuck it back into my pocket then search to see what else I had. Ah some mints, that would help since I was starving. Popping a few in my mouth while my hand was still in my pocket, besides my knife and phone, my keys, my badge and the mints that was it.

Leaning my head back against the wall, I close my eyes, to wait.

My eyes open to total darkness, taking me a second to remember where I was. I stretch then sigh. How do people just sit and do nothing? And how long have I been in here?

I knew I was extremely hungry and thirsty and in desperate need of caffeine but I could have all that when this was over.

Hearing a slight noise outside of the door, I tense as I slide up the wall, checking to make sure the knife was still tucked in the back of my pants. The noise stops, had I been hearing things? A click on the other side, I feel air on my face, the door was opening. A flashlight comes on, I tuck myself ready to launch, once I see the arm holding the flashlight, I swing down with all my might, the light hits the floor, he moans in pain, then I literally attack him launching myself I throw him into the door, we land on the floor, I start swinging connecting with him each time before he manages to push me off. Rolling away from him I feel the knife slide out, I get up seeing the knife I put my foot on it before turning to face him. He stands, growling at me, he sees the cape, he stumbles back a step before another growl.

"You cannot have a cape. You are not the prize, you are not my pretty. I must rid you of existence in the kingdom."

Okay this wasn't going to work so I pull the cape off reaching down for the knife, as I rise to my feet with the knife in my hand he automatically reaches to his back. He growls before lunging at me, raising the knife hoping to imbed it in his stomach but he swings with his arm knocking the knife out of my hand, it hits the wall falling to the floor.

When he turns to see where it lands I throw my feet out knocking him to the floor. He lands on his side with a whoof of air. While he was stunned I quickly get to my feet landing several kicks to his side before he swings his leg, knocking me down on my back. Rolling to the side I push myself up almost to my feet when he growls, knocking me down again. Swinging my legs as he approaches again, this time connecting him with his knee. He growls then screams, I scramble backwards to get out of his reach. Standing with his hands planted on his knees. "You are evil!" Screaming at me as he limps to the door, picking the flashlight up before reaching the door, he picks up something else tossing it at me before slamming the door. I hear the click as it locks.

Letting my breath out as I lay on the floor thinking the next time he comes was going to be brutal. Crawling to find whatever it was he tossed in the room, I find a bag, reaching inside to find a handful of energy bars and two bottles of water. So he had a conscious that was interesting. Or, he still envisioned me as his pretty. Twisting the top of the water off I take a huge gulp before putting the top back on, this had to last who knew how long it will be before he comes back.

Chapter 33

Detective Ron Webb wasn't one to panic, to get frantic but now he was past that point. Where was Grace? She wasn't answering her phone and they couldn't locate it through GPS. Her neighbor hasn't heard anything strange or unusual and her landlord didn't live on premises so he was no use. Her apartment looked normal for Grace, the coffee table had notes and files piled on it, the coffee pot was full with a mug sitting in the sink. No sign of a struggle, no sign of a break in, so she left of her own accord.

But it wasn't like Grace to not keep in touch or answer her phone. Something was wrong.

Taking a chance he goes to the hospital to see Wade, maybe Grace had talked to him before her disappearing act. Nodding at the uniformed guard at Wade's door he enters the room to find him awake but still attached to wires and hoses. "Hey Wade, how are you feeling?"

Wade smiles. "Maybe like I've been in a fight, or maybe at the coliseum fighting the lions." He takes a pause. "Or like a maniac attacked me in the basement of my church, and thankful that I survived. Where's Grace, I haven't heard from her for a couple of days."

Running his hand through his hair. "Yeah that's one of the reasons I'm here. We can't find her. She's not at home she's not answering her phone. No one's heard from her, not even the barista at her favorite coffee shop. I was hoping that she was here or you had talked to her."

Wade raises up with a slight look of panic. "Do you think he abducted her or she went looking for him?"

Ron snorts. "Yeah that's a good possibility especially if she thought of some quirk he may have and went to check it out herself."

Both men smile at the thought before the smiles drop away. "They're taking these monitors off today maybe I can talk them into letting me out to help you look for her."

"No way. You stay here until they release you and then you do exactly what they say. If anything happens to you I'll be the one catching grief from Grace."

Wade settles back against the pillows. "One thing I can do is pray. Please keep in touch and let me know anything you find out."

They knock hands together before Ron leaves the room. So he hasn't heard anything either and the idea that she went off on her own was probably a good one. She had been concentrating on the empty buildings and mentioned she had narrowed the area down but unfortunately she hadn't mentioned the area. Now that he knew no one has seen her he was going to have to tell the captain.

Entering the station to find it unusually quiet, so he asks Sheila. "Hey what's going on, it's awful quiet."

"Meeting in the upstairs conference room. The mayor is showing his backside again." Sheila rolls her eyes.

Taking the stairs two at a time he stands outside the conference room looking through the large glass wall until the captain sees him. He nods his head letting the captain know that he needed to speak with him.

The captain joins him in the hall with Ron leading him away from the window so no one could see them.

"Sorry captain to interrupt but I believe we have a slight problem. No one has seen or heard from Grace for two days now. Not even her boyfriend or the barista. I think she may have gone out on her own to find Hanzor."

The captain clinches his fists. "Then we need to get every available officer on the streets and alert. Do you have any idea where she was going on her theories?"

"She said that she had narrowed the empty buildings down a bit but hasn't shared with me where. I'm sorry captain I thought she was with Wade."

The captain shakes his head. "No don't blame yourself, we all know when she gets an idea she acts first. But let's get looking for her." Opening the door to the conference room he interrupts the mayor, informing his squad of the situation and where to start searching. You could tell the mayor was not pleased with the interruption or the announcement.

Loosing himself in the group of officers that leave the room as quickly as they could, he sees John Green ahead of him. Catching up as they descend the stairs. "Hey John, like to talk to you for a second." Not waiting for an answer as they reach the first floor, Ron grabs his arm, pulling him into an empty interrogation room. Once he had the door closed behind him, he shuts the blinds before turning to the other detective. Moving to stand between John and the door. "I need to know something and I need the truth. Are you the brother of this maniac we're looking for?"

The look on John Green's face said it all. Ron grabs his collar pulling him close. "You tell me where we can find this jerk and you tell me now. He may have Grace."

John's face blanches before turning blood red. He pushes Ron's hands away. "Don't you think if I knew where he was I would get him myself? The boy

has gone bonkers and I have no idea where he is."
Running his hands over his face. "James has always
had some mental issues, according to the doctors
nothing serious, medication would take care of it.
And it did for years until he got his own
apartment. Well we converted the space over the
garage for him. Once he started living away from
mom and dad watching him he quit taking his
medication, he started spending more time alone, he
bought all of this hi-tech computer equipment, he
started going out late at night. We tried to reason
with him but he said he felt better without taking
the medication and he was holding down a job so we
thought maybe he was okay." Pulling a chair down,
he sits. "Then a couple of years ago he pretty much
quit talking and was frequenting a club near the
piers. I followed him a couple of times but all he
was doing was playing a game so I wasn't too
concerned. He started staying away from home longer
and longer until he just quit coming home. We would
check his apartment every few days to see if he's
come to get anything or bring anything back but
nothing has been touched for over a year. When we

started finding the bodies I wondered but it wasn't until Grace started putting a picture together that I figured out it was James." Holding his head in his hands. "If I knew where he was I'd let you know. If I had any idea where he would be I'd go after him."

Feeling sorry for the man that had just wanted to keep his brother close to home, Ron pulls out the other chair and sits down. "Okay let's work together on this. Where do you think he'd go to hide?"

"I've been to every place I can think of, the club he liked, the electronics store he liked to visit, the library, I just don't know."

"What about these abandoned buildings that he left bodies at and the theater? What would they mean to him?"

John shakes his head. "No clue. I even talked to the psychiatrist that he went to, his theory is he's lashing out at family. Yeah family that kept him safe, let him have his own place, yeah that family. Anyway he said that James couldn't and wouldn't do those heinous acts that have been in the paper that was a serial killer probably from another state that found Boston and easy place to find victims."

"And this guy has a license? After we find Grace we'll have her pay him a visit." John smiles for a second. "Okay let's go find your brother and hopefully Grace."

Both men stand, John looks at Ron. "How did you figure out we were related?"

"I didn't Grace did. We saw him at ZoneRoom, she said he looked familiar then compared his photo to yours, no mistaking the resemblance. Sorry."

"Bound to get out sooner or later. Okay let's go."

Leaving the interrogation room together catches the captains attention but Ron just nods at him as they pass, they had work to do.

Chapter 34

Waking to total darkness again not having to wonder where I was. This was day what? Three, four? Losing count of the days wasn't good and surely there were people looking for her now. Surely Ron was, he'd know something was wrong if he hasn't heard from me for days and the captain, he would be worried too.

Crawling off the mattress I make my way to the bag where I had left the water, taking a sip I lean against the wall to eat one of the energy bars. I would need my strength for when he came back.

Thinking back to the day before, he was surprised that I fought back, so he wasn't used to confrontation, maybe he was in a sheltered home. I had the feeling that he had been institutionalized at some point maybe not a lock down but still a facility. Not good with interaction with people so maybe he was born autistic and without medication progressively got worse. So many possibilities and without being able to actually sit down and have a conversation with him, the answers wouldn't come.

The cape didn't work, he appears to still be conflicted on what role I'm supposed to play. His mind is locked in the game and I didn't have anything to make this seem like the game. So confronting him was the only option.

So back to walking the floor, doing lunges, a few sit ups and then a nap. I continued this routine for hours until I felt it was time for sleep. Surprisingly I didn't have trouble going to sleep, since I had met the demon face to face he wasn't invading my dreams any longer. Crawling onto the mattress I close my eyes, falling asleep quickly.

Waking again to the total darkness I go through the same routine I had the day before, so this would be what day five, six? Just as I finished with some sit ups I hear a click near the door, crawling my way over I position myself to be about three feet in front of the door.

Bending just a bit at the waist, rocking back and forth on my feet I was pumping myself up because as soon as that door opens I was jumping.

Finally the door opens at least it sounded like it did, I hear a footstep then another, judging from the sound I think that he's standing in the doorway. I wait until he turns the flashlight on, when the light shines I charge him, knocking him backwards he immediately wraps his arms around me rolling me farther into the room.

We're a tangle of arms and legs, rolling back and forth, neither one of us wanting to let go. Getting one of my arms free I swing out connecting with his face, he groans then let go of me.

We both get up facing each other like prizefighters only this time he has a knife in one hand, not the machete, he's watching me, waiting for me to make a move.

So I start dancing from foot to foot, he watches me, his eyes expressionless. I lunge forward then quickly change direction kicking him in the knee again, he staggers backwards but quickly regains his stance. We continue this dance for what seems forever until he swings his arm in an arc, the blade of the knife barely misses my stomach, I kick at him again as he leans over I punch him in the face. He groans and backups a step, when he looks back up at me, he groans then charges again. This time I lead with the opposite foot but he was ready this time the knife slices my thigh.

With a slight scream, I clamp my hand over the wound. Fury fills my throat, screaming I lunge at him catching him off guard at the last second I kick with both legs connecting with him in the stomach, he falls backwards still gripping the knife. While he was still down I jump on top, pulling my fist back I land a punch in his nose, blood immediately spurts. "And this is for Wade." I punch him again.

With a growl he pushes me off landing on my back he stands over me raising his hands in the air, he screams. Shaking his hands he screams. "Evil! Evil! Revenge!"

Then it hits me, I scoot backwards before raising to my feet. Waiting until his attention is on me. "Vengeance is mine says the Lord." I whisper the words at first.

He stops, he screams, then he turns back slamming the door shut behind him. Turning to me, his face is full of fury. He screams.

"Vengeance is mine says the Lord!" This time I scream the words at him.

He throws his hands over his ears, screaming.

I take the chance. "Do you want to talk now or just scream and fight?" Not letting my guard down in case he wanted to fight more. "By the way, what's your name, I can't keep calling you Hanzor since we aren't in the game."

His lips pressed tight, he shakes his head before answering me. "No Hanzor." Clamping his mouth again before raising his fists. "Fighting is the way to justice." Without a warning he lunges at me knocking me off balance and into the rickety table. My back screams in pain.

I wait until the wave of pain subsides a little before slowly rising to my feet. "For rebellion is like the sin of divination, and arrogance like the evil of idolatry. Because you have rejected the word of the Lord, he has rejected you as king, says the Lord." I scream at him. He clamps his hands over his ears again before screaming. "For we know him who said, "It is mine to avenge; I will repay, the Lord will judge his people." Every time I quote scripture he erupts a little. "When justice is done, it brings joy to the righteous but terror to evildoers."

A fist connects with my nose, I feel blood trickling down my chin, but I wasn't going to wipe it away. I charge at him swinging my legs at the last second, but he turns away and I land on my arm, I hear a crack before the pain radiates. No! I can't fight with a broken arm.

But I still have my feet, getting up slowly refusing to show him my weakness by not holding my arm. I face him before turning quickly kicking my foot in the direction of his stomach, making contact with my boot, he doubles over.

"The fight of the devil..." Rasping out as I take deep breaths.

His hoodie has fallen away from his face, he turns his back to me and I see the handle of the machete poking up. Now if only I could get the machete away.

Before he has a chance to straighten up from the last blow, I deliver another one to his head, he falls to the side holding his head with a moan. Taking advantage of him being on the ground, I kick him in the stomach then the back and then for good measure in the groin. He tightens up into a ball rolling away from me.

While he struggles to get up, I hold my arm, taking deep breaths. "I desire mercy, not sacrifice. For I have not come to call the righteous, but sinners." I whisper as he gets to his feet.

He's breathing as hard as I am, I let go of my arm and hop from foot to foot, ready for the next kick this one I hope would be to his head. Instead he lowers his head ready to charge at me, I sidestep him as he misses me but I manage to get the machete.

When he turns to face me he sees that I'm holding his precious weapon, he steps forward I slash his arm as he holds it out. He pulls backs with a scream his eyes boring into mine and I smile.

We do a dance circling each other, step by step we turn in a large circle. "For with the Lord there is steadfast love, and with him is plentiful redemption."

This time when he screams I'm ready, with all my strength I slice the machete through the air, I connect. With that one swing I slice his throat open, he falls to the ground, holding his neck, his eyes wide full of fear. He drops to his knees, he tries to speak as the blood gushes from his throat. He slowly falls forward, he doesn't move.

Letting the machete fall from my hands before I lower myself to the ground, I reach over to his arm, placing my fingers on his wrist, he was gone.

Quietly I let the tears run down my face, not bothering to wipe them away. I ask forgiveness for taking another life but I feel peace. It was over. And God had watched over me and protected me.

Slowly lowering myself to the ground I let the tears continue before closing my eyes. Waking to a strong odor that wasn't here before I look at

Hanzor lying in a large pool of blood. Then everything rushes back to me.

Turning my head to the door, freedom. Slowly and painfully I get to my feet picking the flashlight up as I wobble toward the door. Reaching for the latch, I close my eyes praying that it will be open. I push the latch down and pull, the door opens and more tears fill my eyes.

Slowly I leave the room, climbing the stairs but when I get to the top I don't have the energy to walk the building to the front door.

Chapter 35

Ron and John walk the alley behind the empty theater, they knew that James had used the back door as much as the front by the tracks so they were focusing on some of the empty buildings that were close, thinking he may have used them also.

With no luck they changed their direction to the pier, John had said that James loved the water and would spend hours sitting on the harbor wall watching the boats. Checking several of the buildings, they came up with nothing except finding a few homeless camps.

Both men were frustrated, they had no clue where to look. John had called his mother to see if my chance James had gone home, but the only thing that accomplished was making his mother cry.

Ron sits down on the wall beside the empty warehouse they had just searched when his phone dings. Looking at the display he jumps up answering the call. "Grace!" There was silence. "Grace!"

"Hey Ron. The building across the street from my apartment." The line goes dead.

Ron stares at his phone before looking at John. "That was Grace, she's at the building across from where she lives." Ron's feet wouldn't move, he was filled with fear on what they would find.

"Well come on man, she needs us." John finally pulls on Ron's arm to make him move.

They exit the pier with Ron waving for a cab and John calling it in. Telling the cab driver to break every law to get them to Congress as fast as he could.

With a smile the driver nods then floors it, pulling in front of Grace's apartment building within fifteen minutes.

Both men jump out with Ron tossing some bills at the driver, they cross the street to the building. Pulling the door open Ron pulls his flashlight out. "Grace!"

They each start scanning the room. "Grace!" John calls from his side of the room.

Reaching the back wall they look around before looking at each other, that's when they hear a weak. "Back here."

Pushing the door open they both enter the room with weapons drawn, scanning the room not seeing anything until a light shines at the doorway at the back of the room.

Running toward the door, Ron reaches her first. She was lying on the floor, blood smeared on her face, slash marks on her side and leg, her pants were blood soaked, her arm was an awkward angle. Ron grabs her and pulls her close. "Grace." He sobs. "Thank God."

John squats down beside them just as the building fills with officers, EMT's and the captain who wipes at his face when he sees her.

Grace looks at John. "I'm sorry John. I'm really sorry."

John stands up and shakes his head. "No Grace I am." He descends the steps to find his brother.

Ron sits down on the floor pulling Grace close. A bottle of water appears in front of him and he helps Grace hold it as she takes a sip. "No coffee?" Her voice is rough.

He laughs. "Not yet."

With a groan she pulls herself to a sitting position, holding her arm, looking around at all the men in blue and a few deceives that were now scouring the place. She spots the captain and smiles, throwing a thumb in the air. He smiles back at her with a wink.

John comes from downstairs, squatting in front of Grace, his eyes a little wet. "I'm so sorry. I should have said something sooner when I suspected it was him." He starts to take Grace's hand before pulling back. "So sorry." He gets up, shoulders hunched walking to the captain.

An EMT touches Ron on the shoulder, he looks up and nods as Grace asks. "What day is it?"

"Sunday, you've been missing for six days."

"What time is it?"

Ron looks at his watch before asking. "Why?" Getting a glare. "It's 10:02 am why?"

Looking up at the EMT. "Can you give us a few minutes?" Struggling just a little, Grace looks at

Ron. "I need to do one more thing then I promise I'll go to the hospital. Okay?"

"What do you need to do?"

"Please I'll explain later, just let me do this." With a weak hug she turns making sure no one was paying attention she skirts the throng of men, going out the side door they had opened.

Taking her time, walking slowly and ignoring the stares from everyone she passed, she made it to Concord Baptist Church. Pulling the heavy doors open, she enters the vestibule to hear the choir finishing. She opens the door to the sanctuary just as Wade starts speaking. Slowly she walks down the aisle, crying harder the closer she gets to the front. Wade stops speaking when he sees her, he descends the pulpit meeting her as she reaches the altar.

"My God. Grace." He wraps his arms around her just as she falls.

Looking into his eyes, she sees love there, she sees her future. "Hey, you look pretty good."

Holding her tight he whispers a prayer of thankfulness and gratitude in her ear adding for healing. When he raises his head, tears are streaming down his face she sees faces appearing over his shoulder as she passes out. "I need to ask for forgiveness, I took a life."

Ron pushes his way through the people until he was leaning over Wade's shoulder. "EMT's are outside, want to help me clear a way for them?"

Wade nods leaning down and kissing Grace on the forehead before looking up. "The EMT's need to get in, can we make a way for them? And thank you all for your prayers."

As the people back away a few pat Wade on the shoulder, he thanks them as the EMT's approach with a gurney. After loading her on, Wade turns to the congregation. "Folks I'm leaving the service in your hands." With one hand firmly clasped on the gurney, Wade escorts Grace to the ambulance.

Chapter 36

Four days later Grace opens her eyes to find herself in the hospital with her arm in a cast, bandages tightly wrapped her thigh and other arm and eyes that won't open completely.

"Well sleeping beauty finally wakens."

Grace looks to her side to see Ron sitting in one of the four chairs in the room, Wade was sitting in another with the captain and John filling the others.

"Wow is this a party or what?" Her voice was rough and raspy, she desperately needed coffee or the glass of water that appears.

Wade comes to stand beside her taking her hand he kisses her knuckles. "We've been keeping watch. We were worried."

Giving him the best smile I could. "Thank you."

The captain clears his throat making Wade lean down. "They need to talk to you I'll be back after they're done." Kissing her again he leaves with a wave at the door.

As the captain pulls a notebook from him pocket I hold my hand up. "First things first. Coffee then food then coffee and then I'll talk."

John jumps up. "I'll take care of that." Leaving the room quickly.

Laying my head back against the pillows, Ron slowly raises the head of the bed so I could talk to them.

"I really hate to make you do this, but until you can come into the office to write your report we need to know what happened." The captain looks a little uncomfortable.

Waving my good arm. "No problem, but it may be easier to tape than write it down."

Ron holds his phone up. "Ready to go. Start talking and if we have any questions we'll interrupt."

Taking another sip of water. "Okay. Ever since this case started I've had this creepy feeling when I was in my apartment, I pushed it off as just the case until I noticed a light on in the building across the street. He'd been there the whole time and he was watching me." Seeing the look of horror on both their faces. I walk them through the whole thing from entering the building finding where he had been standing as he watched me to finding his home in the basement. After I explained it all including his obsession with me and why, to the horror when he found that I had green eyes instead of brown to him losing himself totally in the game that was his reality.

The captain clears his throat. "You said you threw him off a little, how did you do that?"

"Quoting scripture. Every time I said a verse, he screamed, he pulled his hair, he lost his head a little and attacked, that's how I got the upper hand."

A throat clears and we all turn to see John standing in the doorway with a large brown bag from the deli and a tray of coffees. "I can explain that. Growing up we went to church faithfully, we could quote the Bible backwards and forwards. But when he started showing signs of a mental disability he would cringe whenever he heard scripture, the psychiatrist that mom had started taking him to said it would be better to not bring Christianity into the house. So we quit going."

"I need to know who this psychiatrist is. From what you've said his license needs to be pulled." I hold my hand out hoping for the coffee but get the bag instead.

As I dig in they discuss the way I handled the whole situation just like I wasn't there, but since I was devouring as much food as I could I tuned out.

Finally the captain turns to me with his stern look. "Grace I commend you for your actions and for bringing down a killer. But. You ever take off on your own again like that without telling anyone your plans, you will be suspended. Or worse." Since my mouth was full I nod my understanding. "And you and Webb are now a team. You will be working on these cases together. At his request."

My eyes open wide, I swallow the food before trying to speak. "Seriously? The man that made fun of my choice of careers, the man that was complaining about the demons that were taking over, he wants to be partnered with me to handle these cases?" I see three nods.

"Huh, imagine that."

"And." The captain looks at John who nods. "John would like to be a liaison whenever you need him."

"Wow a whole team now. Can I just tell them what to do while I sit in my office and drink coffee?" When I said that I hold my hand out for a cup which Johns provides.

Getting three smiles the captain answers my question. "Absolutely. Not." Tucking his notebook back into his pocket. "Ron send me that recording please. Grace I'm glad that you weren't hurt any worse than you were and I do not want to see you in the office for another week at least."

Thanking the captain as he leaves I turn to the two men left. John clears his throat a couple of times before he speaks. "Grace I'm so sorry for what my brother did. I wish there was a way I could make up for what he did."

I could tell that this was eating him up, so I motion for him to come closer. "John this has nothing to do with you or your family in any way. Your brother had a serious mental disability and unfortunately the doctor that was taking care of him didn't give him the correct treatment. People like your brother lose themselves in their fantasies mistaking them for reality until it consumes them and without the correct treatment it escalates into what he did, in his mind he thought he was doing right, he was making sacrifices for a treasure the way he was instructed to do. He thought he was doing right so please don't blame yourself. I know that you were a good brother to him and I'm glad that I'm the one that stopped him and not you."

John nods his head. "I hear you, it's just going to be hard for a while." Leaning over he kisses my cheek. "And I'm glad you're okay." With a nod to both of us he leaves the room.

From where he was sitting in one of the chairs Ron says. "It's going to take him some time."

I nod. "Yep. For me too."

"We'll be there for you."

I nod again before I ask. "Think we can find me a place just as close to the office that I have now?"

His eyes widen. "Why you want to move?"

Thinking hard, do I? "Yes I do. Maybe one of those brownstones behind the station with two bedrooms and I can have pets." I smile at the thought. "Maybe a cat or a little dog I can bring into the office in a bag like celebrities do?"

With a deep laugh. "Anything."

Wade re-enters the room with a smile and another cup of coffee. "Ah I see you've eaten and have coffee, so I'll just toss this one."

"You do and I'll never speak to you again." Holding my hand with the best glare my swollen eyes will let me give.

Ron gets up leaning over he gives me a soft kiss on the forehead. "I'll let you two duke it out over the coffee." Shutting the door softly behind him as he leaves.

Wade sits on the edge of the bed. "We need to talk."

"If you're going to give me another lecture, than no we're not, I've had enough of those. The only thing I'm saying is when you were missing I realized how much you mean to me."

With a huge smile, Wade takes my hand. "That's what I was going to say. So can we call ourselves exclusive now? I don't see anyone else and neither do you, unless it's the cat or dog you're talking about getting."

"Um, how are the ladies with daughters and granddaughters in church going to take that."

"With a grain of salt and God's blessing."

Thank you for taking the time to read Watching Grace, I sincerely hope that you enjoyed the books in the two other series available. If you've missed any of them, they are available through Amazon and Barnes & Noble. And if you enjoyed this book, you may enjoy the Miss Margaret Christian Adventures also.

REVIEWS! REVIEWS! REVIEWS! Indie authors rely on their reviews, to see how well their work is received, whether they have an audience and of course for sells. Please take time to go back and review this book and any other of the L.G. Blankenship books.

Sam Fields Series

Illusions

Wicked Witness

Lost Decade

Force of One

Misplaced Intentions

Fools Treasure

Relative Involvement

Crushed Dreams

Miss Margaret Adventures

Made in the USA
Columbia, SC
20 November 2017